Rodney Hall

CAPTIVITY CAPTIVE

A Fireside Book
Published by Simon & Schuster Inc.
New York   London   Toronto   Sydney   Tokyo

Fireside
Simon & Schuster Building
Rockefeller Center
1230 Avenue of the Americas
New York, New York 10020

*First Fireside Edition, 1989
Published by arrangement with Farrar, Straus & Giroux, Inc.
FIRESIDE and colophon are registered trademarks
of Simon & Schuster Inc.*

*Designed by Cynthia Krupat
Manufactured in the United States of America*

1 3 5 7 9 10 8 6 4 2 Pbk.

Library of Congress Cataloging in Publication Data

ISBN 0-671-67441-2 Pbk.

For John Hooker

Laymen often ask men of learning
why Adam did not first cover his mouth,
the part that had eaten the apple,
rather than his loins.

—WILLIAM LANGLAND
Piers Ploughman

Captivity Captive

There were crows in his eyes when he came right
out with it, confessing that he had been the murderer.
You could see them flapping in there. And now and again
the glint of a beak. You can't tell me anything about
crows I don't already know at eighty. Nor about him,
either.

It's no good saying, like Norah used to, that I'm the
one who always let his imagination run riot. You ought
to have seen the hungry fluttering in that look of his,
those scavengers working away at the rotten flesh of
corpses long dead and mostly forgotten.

Poor old bloke, the dill. Dismal is what you'd call him.
Dismal the whole of his life. I can be sure of this because
I knew him for all but the first couple of years of it.

He spoke the word *murder* in a croak. Even this came
crow-sweet, what with Ireland still hanging on him, afraid
to let him go, counting every one of her children (me

included) and mad for numbers. *Marder*, he said it. Then, on account of being in his deathbed, which this time was permanent enough, the wings in his coaxing eyes fluttered and folded, twitched out again, and really did fold.

He looked peaceful; the picture of a man who has confessed his soul's torment and expects eternal absolution just for the saying of it. But I knew he was raging with excitement. What he always promised himself he would do, he had done. He never thought he'd rouse enough courage. And now here he was, flat on his back, being listened to by an inspector of police. Oh yes, he had gone that high. Not just Jim, our local constable, but an inspector down from Sydney on a special visit to nobody else.

Poor coot had scored the top brass and you could see how it set his blood spinning with grief that he hadn't made this occasion when he was younger and might have enjoyed it to the full. But there was no one else to blame, so he shut his mouth and shut his eyes and made such a good impression of being gratified that, if the whole town didn't know him for a wowser, a witness might have been pardoned for thinking he was a drunk. This excitement put the colour back into his skin. He looked as if he might not die, after all. One word, *murder*, bringing him to life again. I thought: We shall be laughing over this for years to come.

Then he spoke some more, the flurry of crows now getting to his voice, muffling and rattling it.

"That was when I bashed the horse's brains in with the bludgeon-stick," he said.

Those exact words. He said them in front of us, even knowing us the way he did. Also knowing what we knew about him. Can you believe? But I don't think he realized the inspector's question might have been several questions, in each case tricky enough. Barney was a dill.

"Why? That's what I don't understand. Why?" was what the inspector put to him.

"Why?" he bellowed, eyes still shut, the fast blood giving him strength he had no use for any longer. He was panicking. His mouth hung open with his tongue humping and writhing inside, a fat white slug working its way over the question.

Even my mother, who walked round in a cloud of the darkness she gave out, couldn't have touched Barney Barnett for resentment at that moment, though I am convinced he thought the question *Why?* simple enough, the point being that he never expected to have to answer questions. He planned to do all the talking needed. Finally he got his white slug past the boulder and grumbled: "This is 1956, don't you know?" Then, as I understood it, his dim cross-grained mind got onto the fact that if he wanted to die famous he would have to fight for it. He gathered energy during those failing minutes and spoke out of an irritable hunger, still with his eyelids kept down so no one could see in to where the scavengers were busy. "I'm not talking about no bloody horse, I'm talking about him. Him and his sisters!"

The bedsheet had a bit of cottage lace along the edge, worked by his grandma, more than likely, whose needle-craft had made her a local identity. Like a baby, he hooked his finger through a hole where some stitches were coming adrift.

Barney felt ashamed of his granny and grandpa, I might mention, both of them being English; they came in on his father's side and he swore he was his mother's son. So he was. She gave birth to him in Ireland, the country of his heart, and he never outgrew it. In that way of being boastful about his Irishness, there was some sympathy between him and my brother Michael, this cannot be denied. But with Barney it was a snivelling don't-put-me-off-my-stroke-or-I-might-miss-it-altogether kind of thing, whereas Michael bounced around boyish with cheerfulness and forever working things out by getting them wrong. Michael, who was one of the victims he just claimed to have killed fifty-eight years previous to hanging on by a hole in his English grandma's sheet.

Our family didn't bother speaking like Irishmen, not even Pa or Mum. We were Australians with a healthy scorn for any superstition brought out here from the old country. Unless you mean the Church. We went to mass, all but Ellen, the youngest of the murder victims.

A priest was with us at the deathbed. He was the one to keep murmuring in the inspector's direction: Don't you think he's tired? Don't you think I should take over now? Don't you think the last rites will settle his mind? Surely we should let the poor man turn his eyes to God before too late?

The old priest, Father Gwilym, would never have cut such a feeble figure. He'd have been master of the occasion, with his purple stole on, critical of the crucifix and candles already set in place by the householder, and sprinkling holy water with casual flicks.

This new man fumbled when dabbing the consecrated oil at Barnett's nostrils. Did he so deeply dread the mortal contact? The pad then touched eyes, swollen lips, and ears burning with the sin of pride. The words of absolution escaped him in a voice little better than an apology, the same voice he found to say thank you when handed a dry specimen of lemon on which to cleanse his fingertips before accepting the towel folded in his honour. He stepped back a pace and committed a quiet sigh.

We were a great age. I looked at the others and they looked at me. Poor Barney, said our looks which we made no attempt to conceal, the fool thinks he was big enough to plan a crime so famous it is printed in encyclopedias. Sly even then, he let his eyes show only a moment, unable to resist checking if he had outwitted us. Black wings gave a twitch in there. Finding the effort too taxing, perhaps, his gaze sank to wander from one to the other of his hands as they crawled about his chest like sightless creatures.

The Sydney inspector switched an unspoken question

to us, but was offered no satisfaction, so he addressed the dying man again, politely controlling any sign of how exasperated he had become.

"Look, Mr Barnett, you need to tell me something we don't already know. You're going to need to tell me something new, something only the murderer could possibly tell. I am not empowered," he explained almost pathetically, "to take your word on such an important matter."

Startled crows fluttered a moment, but Barney wisely let his lids droop once more. He never could make an artifice stick. Yet he managed quite well at having it seem that they drooped under the weight of injustice which would not admit he knew whether or not he was guilty, would not allow him to sacrifice his reputation to the ultimate penalty of notoriety.

"If I could accept just anyone's word," the inspector grumbled, "where would we be? I suggest you cast your mind back to the night of the murders."

By way of answer, the parasitic hands sucked at each other in a desperate effort to rise to an occasion suddenly difficult beyond all expectation.

"I need only one thing, one detail unknown till now. That may be enough to clinch the matter. You must have thought about it for years."

Oh the poor fellow, laid out to die with his lies. And us gathered round his bed already putting him in mind of hell. We were the problem, no doubt about that. We were the ones he had not planned on seeing, the survivors, so square and blank that the gaps between us stood solid as the absent three who had been murdered, Norah, Ellen, and Michael.

Our mother had died of grief because she could not learn to weep, any more than she'd been able to learn to laugh. She set her curse to work throughout this occasion because she predicted the murderer would never be allowed to die without confessing for all the world to condemn him. She breathed out her expectancy, simple as air. We breathed it in. We knew she had come.

But the chief figure towering over us and taking up most of the available space, as rigid and dark as basalt rock, was our dead father, seated on his dead black stallion. His hands, blunt and hairy as lion paws, one crossed over another while clasping the reins loosely—I felt my own hands the same, though they only held the brim of my funeral trilby—and the apprentice corpse struggled to disengage his finger from a hole in the lace. The horse exchanged weight, left haunch to right. Father's hat rose an inch, enough to touch the ceiling, and sank again.

My good humour had the power to kill. I could see an end to the misery and complications.

Even with a ghost filling that bare room, the coward in bed braved his fate and refused to give in. He stuck to his story, eyes squeezed tight against fear, knowing as he must that absolution for his other sins would count for nothing in heaven if he died under the weight of this last lie, plus trying to steal the priest's forgiveness from the sinner who truly needed it. Meanwhile, the priest himself remonstrated against any further investigation, at least having enough wit to see the saved soul might fall into subsequent error.

"I used a bludgeon-stick to bash their heads in," Barney's feeble voice insisted, as if this were no different from the statement he made before. "I swung it with both me hands."

Pa's horse arched its tail to achieve that fastidious ceremony unequalled by any other beast.

The inspector straightened up. You couldn't help being sorry for him, so disillusioned and frustrated he looked. He might have paced the room had there been space. We watched him, which is to say all except Pa, who watched only me. I knew my father's expression without checking, the dead eyes indifferent as they had been when he whipped me, indifferent as they had been when I first ploughed the fifteen-acre paddock and believed I had done well. Then I did check. Yes, exactly as I thought. He was waiting to see if I would tell what I knew.

Can you imagine how it felt to have such power over him I could keep him sitting on his stallion, hold his gaze, and refuse to say anything?

"They were my marders," Barney's voice insisted contemptibly. "All mine."

Pa was a sad giant, as big as any pair of us except Jerry, Jerry having taken after him in size. When we were young men he liked to wrestle us two at a time. We could never hold him down. I don't believe he knew how much we hated him for this. I think he hoped we enjoyed the intimacy, in a life offering not much warmth you could relish. The palpable heaviness of contact, as I remember it, was made stranger still by sensuousness.

He never laughed, my father. So at one stage I considered him insane. As for us, we laughed a lot. I suppose he hated our laughter as much as we hated his wrestling matches. But this was not the worst of it. He suffered terrible attacks of rage, which Barney Barnett, incidentally, would never have known about. He'd beat you to the ground, then strap you on a bed-end and flog you for no reason he could explain through the froth filling his mouth. I do not wish to make it sound as if we thought our childhood hell; no, we accepted our parents as fairly typical and conforming to the general rule. What I say about my father applies, more or less, to my mother too, but I shall try to account for her later.

Pa said he never wanted us to leave home.

You might have thought we were a burden, all ten children having survived in those times when you could usually reckon on losing at least one in three within its first twelve months. But no, he raged against us if we tried to skip the farm. When I was nine, my eldest brother William, at twenty, asked permission to go up north and seek work on the railway line. The request alone was enough and a proof of treachery. Pa crushed him—I witnessed this—smashed his ribs and collarbone, took him by one leg and growled, "I'll break it now if you like, or wait till you try giving me the slip and break it then." William, being already proud as a man should be, swore and lay silent. But he gave in. That night he went for Pa with a butcher's knife, gashing his shoulder, but the old man beat him up so badly he never fully found himself again. He came round and got better. But it wasn't the Willie we knew—jaunty on horseback, a squire for the women hereabouts—who ate at our table and drudged in the fields. He emerged from that fight a different shape, flesh hung heavily on him and his spirit went a separate way. Previously Willie had been the one we turned to when we didn't turn to Norah with our troubles.

After this I used to tell myself, under the blanket at night, that I had better grow up as quick as possible and practise running. I couldn't wait to cut loose. But the way life happened, I need not have worried. It makes you laugh to think of: Pa didn't want me to be confined at home. He wanted me to learn about the world outside. Not like Danny, whom he threw out when the time came, but not like the others either. You'd think I was a reproach to him, a reminder of some person or event greater than myself. That's how it seemed to me at the time. Only for my mother wanting me to stay, I believe I might never have been around the place on 26th December 1898. If so, I would probably have died of common old age long ago, I dare say, with no punishment to sustain me.

Now you have a rough idea of Daniel Murphy, the father. But let me give you a few more facts while I'm at it. Born in Tasmania, though he never had papers to prove anything by, he stood six feet ten inches in his socks and weighed twenty-six stone of solid graceless strength, everything about him being dense and thick. His wrists! It amazes me to think of them. Nothing could hurt him. Once, the winch let fly when we were hauling logs and the heavy handle spun over, knocking him off his feet. We had hopes, I can tell you, but he got up and grabbed hold of it like a chicken farmer wringing a bird's neck. He never even showed a bruise that I can remember. We couldn't help being proud of him.

Johnnie and I used to have a joke when the first tractors went to work down our way: "Useless bloody things," we'd say, "you could run over Pa with one of them and he'd get up and kick it in the arse." That was the kind of joke we used to make, while Norah would come flying over to tell us we should be ashamed of ourselves, but immediately forget and veer off at a tangent: "Just look at your hair, Johnnie! Have you been pulled backwards through a hedge, then? Sit down and I shall cut it for you so the girls'll all see you for the handsome lad you are. My, but you're growing," she'd prattle affectionately. She might begin to comb his thatch right then, while he sat docile in the power of her happiness, and she'd take the shears to it till one of the younger girls limped indoors crying, so she'd have to fix that drama with a dab of perfume or some small treat kept tucked in her pinafore pocket. Back she'd come to find young Johnnie had skipped away and she'd laugh, threatening to leave him lopsided for a week with half his hair cut and half shaggy.

Our childhood was filled with happiness, with flights of swans and hailstorms at night when the clouds were lit like giant flowers overhead, heavy with honey and rooted to the soil by lightning. Life was, in its unrepeatable way, perfect. You could say it stayed like that. Even to the murders.

When Polly got married we were glad to lumber the butcher with her calamity of foolishness. Polly did not see what you or I might see. She saw only herself and her necessities. She couldn't talk but the gossip hopped out, fluttered and flopped like amphibious creatures losing their tails but almost too transparent to be seen at all. The crops will be ruined if it doesn't rain soon, you might say, at which she'd clench her hands in despair and reply: "I suppose this is your way of telling me I shan't get my new bonnet I need!"

The butcher had to be a bible-basher himself, or he'd never have got the notion she was marriable. They had Connemara forebears in common. Our grandparents had not survived long enough for us to actually know them. Except Mum's father, who was recollected by Polly from when she was a little girl. He had white whiskers stained brown in patches, she once told me, and flabby lips he couldn't keep still from trembling. Even his voice, which was very deep, shuddered while he spoke. I dare say William would have remembered him too if he hadn't been beaten up that way and gone partly blank in his mind; I had never thought to ask him before too late. So Polly was my only link with someone I might, for all I knew, take after.

As for my parents, they could not be asked to recall simple things like names and appearances.

If they had not found each other, it is difficult to think how either Pa or Mum would ever have married. As he was a giant, so was she a giant too, with bones on a big scale overlaid by hard fat. The very day of the murders, she pushed me into a corner till I made her a promise I'd keep out of the bookmakers' clutches, and I knew, as a person does know, just the push of her weight by itself was beyond my strength to resist. So I did not try. Sometimes I enjoyed being reliable. She was only two inches shorter than Pa.

I should say I am an ordinary five feet nine inches and, at that time, weighed not much more than half what she did, though I was thought a great athlete in the district. The uniqueness of their marriage lay in more than physical bulk. More even than the sharing of inherited prejudices. They were suited in a deeper way. Since neither one felt any tenderness for us once we grew out of the baby stage (except perhaps for me as Mum's favourite), they faced no recrimination when their eyes met. They exchanged thanks for this closeness, in their daily routines,

by silences chock full of accepting the rightness of Mum
to be mother and Pa to be father. They believed in themselves so completely I doubt if they considered there could
be any other kind of household. You may not think this
possible. But they had few friends, no one visited us, and
they went nowhere except to market or to mass.

I shall have more to say about the annual picnic races
at Yandilli and about our Polly's marriage to the butcher,
both of which were exceptions, times when they were
seen out together.

I must add here that my parents' lives were upright
and decent. They never coveted their neighbours' house,
nor did they desire his servant, nor his handmaid, they
never committed adultery (who with?) nor stole nor
took the name of the Lord in vain. But when we come to
the sixth commandment, murder is not so simply set
aside.

My father's father had built the farmhouse and fenced
the paddocks, and he was the one who hammered the
name of the place on copper and screwed it to the wall
beside the front door: PARADISE. He saw here the chance
of a life free from the poverty of his youth.

We used to hear about our grandparents only on ritual
occasions, such as the renewal of fenceposts. "My own pa
split these posts," Pa might say, and look them over criti-
cally. "Not a bad job," he'd observe, "for a clumsy bloke."
We'd sweat at digging, at lugging the new posts laid
ready months before, mopping faces with our forearms,

and we'd lean on the long shovels. Then he might add: "Very particular he was, my pa, about keeping a straight line, him and his spools of thread."

Likewise, on Mum's side it was often household work that brought Grandma to mind. "My ma," she'd burst out in her resentful way, "always reckoned she rolled the flaky pastry twenty times with twenty lots of lard, if you please." Having said this, she'd look round ferociously, challenging us kids to judge her by her mother's performance, though we'd never known the old lady. Then she'd go vague again and pound away at the dullness of what she had begun.

A famous photograph was taken at Paradise in 1880, the year our Ellie was born, who was destined to be one of the victims. This was also the year they caught the outlaw Ned Kelly, tried him, and hanged him. The trial confirmed that he had become the most famous man of his time, not just as a bushranger but as a spokesman— by his deeds—for the underdog. I was small at the time, so I remember nothing of Ned Kelly, but I remember the photograph being taken and how it terrified me. The photographer liked the look of our twenty and lobbed in one day to ask Pa's permission to set up his scene down there by the creek near where it flows into the sea. He took a fancy to the line of swamp mahoganies and that nice flat patch looking the right spot for a likely camper to choose.

Let me tell you what I recall about the occasion and

then explain how the photograph came out. I have a copy, so I can describe it for you in detail.

First came a funny feeling in our house. Mum asked, while she bent over her meal, who was the fellow in the gig that came bowling across our yard? Pa stuffed his mouth full of potato and seemed like he wasn't about to give a straight answer. I sensed something special was happening, because Norah gave a swift motherbird look around the table, to be certain not one of us young ones would pipe up and put ourselves in the line of a swinging fist. We kept our eyes on our plates. I mostly found myself fascinated by the crazing of the china under its glaze, the entire plate a web of faint brown cracks that still were not cracks on the surface. Here and there, chips round the rim were the same discolour. Mum didn't ask again, as I recollect, but Pa swallowed what he had in his mouth and pushed his dish away to give room for the grand word he had chosen to share. Photography, he said, pronouncing it photo*graphy*. That out there was a photo*graphy* man come with his gig to take a picture at the bottom of our twenty, he explained. And suddenly everything was all right. "I can't put it," he added, "more fine than that."

Mum mustn't have voiced her opinion of photography, or we would certainly have known it. Later, when her Polly had a wedding portrait taken by a friend of the butcher's who was an amateur with the camera, she let fly her bottled-up fury against the sinfulness of graven images: photographs were the work of the Devil and unnatural. What happened, she wished to be informed on this later occasion, when your image went inside that little black box, because if it didn't *go* inside, how did it get there for the print to show it afterwards? Graven things, they were, she insisted. Thou shalt not make to thyself the likeness of any thing that is on earth or in heaven above, she quoted. But we just thought this was because of the many times Father O'Shaughnessy repeated the commandments in his sermons; also to remind us she, at least, was taking his instructions to heart. He was a priest whom she never tired of comparing with the new men, always to their dis-advantage.

So, perhaps Mum held her feelings in, as she so often did, letting them stew away and build up a good head of pressure for when she chose to blow her top and could muster a scorching catalogue of instances where life had let her down.

Anyhow, a week later (I know a Sunday came between because she had her say to the priest and most likely put forward some unexpectedly curly theological knots for him to unravel), Michael came running over the paddock to where the rest of us were mucking around with the poddies, and just stood there, hands on hips, jack-knifing, so winded he was. When he swallowed his breath, some words got out. These were chiefly warnings about how careful we'd have to be if we wanted to be in on it at all. The end was that we crept after him along the fence going down the home paddock and in among those she-oaks at the bottom. There we could stand up and not be seen from the kitchen, so we picked our way through the clump of little paperbarks, which I loved for growing so close together you could hardly squeeze between. We came out at the swamp, of course, and pushed on a little way to the corner post. You'd never imagine what we saw.

First I noticed a fellow in a white shirt with his back to us, a fair way off, tightening the surcingle on one of his horses. I mean, how did he get his horses into our twenty for a start! There were a whole lot of them too, maybe six or seven, and all loaded with who knows what, saddles and packsaddles, weighed down they were, and standing patient, shaking flies off their faces, watching him with the lead horse and that surcingle giving him trouble. He had a new hat on, by the look of it. This was what gave him away. He didn't know a thing about those horses. He had the wrong hat. Only then did I see what else was happening. A tiny black tent stood over to the sliprails side, plus a pair of man's legs stuck out under it. And then an arm poked up from the black material and waved. I was about to pinch Danny, because we were special mates at that time, but Michael put his hand across my face before I could make a move or let out a sound. I smelt something stinky on his fingers, but I couldn't wriggle free. I think I must have turned to Norah to have me released when I saw what Norah was looking at. Over where those paperbarks cut in along the fence at the bit we always had to check because that was the wire the cattle generally had a go at, also being the weakest stretch by bad luck, as Pa said while Mum put in her two-bob's-worth about Satan, some Aborigines were creeping up quiet as cats. Most of them had nothing on that I could see. One must have been wearing trousers, though, because later he took a stone out of his pocket. Creeping up like somebody on springs. We watched from the side. Their spears were sticking out a long way in front of them, each spear maybe twice as long as the hunter who held it. And all aimed at that white shirt. The points wobbled like snakes ready to strike. Any minute they would whisk through the air and bury themselves in a man's back. Hat or no hat, and despite his horses being on our place when they shouldn't have come past the first gate, I couldn't help it but I had to yell out.

Mike got me and nearly strangled me. Norah had to fight him off. But too late. I'd already yelled *Watch out!* in that kind of scream a kid can give which carries a mile on a windless day.

One of the horses played up and jumped sideways against the fence, the little black tent went mad with some fellow inside struggling to get out, while the chap in the hat knocked it off his own head and the Aborigines just sat down where they were and laughed around their broken teeth. I never saw an Aborigine laugh before. But they laughed so much they gave themselves bellyache. And then, of course, came Pa thundering over the rise from where he'd been watching, already struggling to unbuckle his belt and pull it out from the loops on his trousers. We were for it! And I was the guilty one who had opened my big mouth.

But something even more amazing happened. The fellow from under the tent tried to catch Pa by the arm, a thing no sensible man ever did, and Pa swung round to fell him, but changed his mind just in time. The fellow shouted out to the hunters, who gathered their spears and shuffled up, then wandered back in a lazy way among the trees. He called to Pa, who was already on his way towards us again: "No harm done." I shall always remember those words. It became one of my own sayings from that day on. No harm done. Pa, ready to kill us, stormed over. If you watch, he roared and choked, you'll see a real live photo*graphy* took.

The picture was put up in the photographer's shop down in Bunda. I saw it there many years afterwards, still the same shot, and that's when I bought my copy. It was called *Caught Unawares 1880. From the studio of Charles Bailey*. Bailey had painted across his shop window: NEVER-FADING PORTRAITS, A MOST APPROPRIATE WEDDING PRESENT.

Sure enough, the print shows black men with spears poised, only a few steps behind their unsuspecting victim, who is not doing up a surcingle at all but unloading a tent and gold-fossicking tools. The horses are too fresh to fool anybody but a rookie. Even the gold pans and sieve, even the shovels, don't look as if they'd ever seen dirt till that moment of being propped artfully against a heap of tentpoles.

So the picture was the kind of thing you purchased in those days for sending home to Ireland, to show what pioneers you were, and snakes not the worst of it by any means. The hat, incidentally, comes out quite all right in the print and doesn't look too new. But what I can't get over is how scrubby our twenty is made out to be. I never would have credited this unless I'd unearthed the very picture for you.

I think of the paddock as spiky grass with lots of cowpats, hoof holes, and scattered dead wood gone white and hollow as bone. The usual. But here it's a mess of fallen branches and ragged trees. And now I realize something awful. This could not be our twenty, not with that big spotted-gum just to the right. No spotted-gums were left there at all. Ironbark, yes, and a couple of wollybutts, but no spotted-gums, because Grandpa had laid down the rule that they were treacherous, being so tall and straight with so few branches and small roots. You don't want them blowing down in a storm on top of your good beasts, the saying went. No, this was not our property. After me letting out that yelp, they must have gone elsewhere to try again for some atmosphere. I don't remember this. I remember the photography being at our place.

I put the print away, but I wasn't satisfied.

That spotted-gum was the clue. It haunted me. I felt I knew the tree from somewhere. Then I had it: the base of this tree was where they found Norah's body. *Caught Unawares* had been taken eighteen years before the real murder, acted out by native people with no harm left in them, to show us what we might make of the affair when it struck at the same spot. Mum went to the Deaseys' for her lying-in with Ellie when the photographer called by to show us his work. I don't know why she went. She gave birth to all the rest of us at home. But Ellen was born over at Mrs Deasey's.

What a commotion she made when she did eventually see the photograph, though. This was in Bunda and a long time later when Ellie was already walking. As a treat, we'd gone all the way there for the big Boxing Day races, instead of just to Yandilli. Mum was doubly out-raged when she discovered they could make copies, as many as anyone wanted from a single negative. This seemed more wonderful to us than anything you could imagine. But she told Pa: "Those savages are going to get ideas from this, mark my words, they'll come round here spearing your own daughters for twopence, you and your photography man giving them ideas best left unthought."

They were, of course, the blacks meant in Blacks Creek. I always thought it was for a person called Mr Black when I was young. I'd supposed Mr Black might have been here before Grandpa chose the creek bank for our house site. Not till I went to classes with the nuns after I got my job did I ask about history. The answer turned my world on its head for a moment, because I had never known any other place and I suddenly got the impression I didn't know this place either.

Before going further, something ought to be said on the subject of our church at Cuttajo. The priest, Father

Gwilym, was Mum's pet complaint. First because he wasn't a patch on her Father O'Shaughnessy, and second because he wasn't Irish. Father Gwilym was a foreigner from Wales whose passion and ambition was to have music in his church good enough to serve God and glorify the Holy Virgin. Accordingly, he taught the boys to sing and the girls to play the violoncello and the organ. Every mass, we had music on some scale. One service in particular left me with the feeling the sulky floated all the way home. Aged about fifteen, I suppose, because my voice had long since broken, I felt heaven all around me. The harmonies showed me the bush as I had never seen it before: full of light. Our sulky rolled through the glare, smooth and silent. I wanted to sing, but felt embarrassed by my croaking voice and those blurting deep notes which sounded like someone unknown to me, or more like some thing, perhaps, escaping my mouth.

We were all afraid of provoking Pa to violence. Years before, I had sung in the choir and served at the altar. Now I was a renegade who secretly scorned religion. But I thought these harmonies, on strings and organ, sublime. "Did you see," said Mum, spitting dust, "the church had more Judies sawing away than god-fearing worshippers?" I heard this with shock. "Like a pub on Bedlam night," she added, while I flicked the horse with the reins.

Some years later that same sulky was given to Bill McNeil as a wedding gift for taking Polly off our hands. It was the one, patched up and kept going, which he habitually brought to our place when they visited (though we knew full well they owned a new model for deliveries) and which he lent to Michael on the fateful night for driving the girls to the Cuttajo dance.

This much was true, those same church players played our waltzes and our Dashing White Sergeant at the Cuttajo Hall of a dance night. Older though they had grown, and no matter how many children they gave birth to, they always hung together and never gave up their love of the thing. They were the ones who had gone home from the hall when Michael and Norah and Ellen arrived late, to be met by a locked door and not a chink of light anywhere but from the houses in that part of town.

Pa was afraid of hell. Hell was the one thing he was afraid of. But he hated mass. So he went only as often as he thought he must to keep in favour with heaven. Mum used it as a weapon against him. She had two weapons: her mulish ability to obstruct events by doing nothing; and the everlasting punishment that awaited almost all of us almost all the time, but never her. This is not to say she felt safe, far from it; she simply took good care not to overstep the mark. In fact she was obsessed, I suppose you'd have to say, with the threat of evil. There were times when I looked at her big solid face hoping it would show some expression and all I saw were the eyes flying wide with a lust for fear, which she would burst rather than show us. Even her acceptance of the inevitable drudgery of a cocky's wife, expressed in that flat voice, those large simple gestures of not caring, were outward signs of the purgatory she created in her head for us all.

When my mother came into a room she soaked up the light. It wasn't just her shadow. She exhausted everything alive and sunny.

This was how Polly came to be her favourite daughter and Norah the one she mistrusted. She loved us all at some time or another, of course, though she had a clumsy way of showing it. But Norah, as her warmth grew too strong to be stifled, saw the milder side of her less and less.

Yet, perversely, I was Mum's pet among the boys; and what this did to my father I shall never know, but he made special efforts to correct any false impression I might have got by treating me with particular strictness—not the same bashing William had come in for, but steely reminders that my transgressions against his rule of law were never to be forgotten and, though to voice any such threat would have been beneath him, would eventually catch up with me, thanks to his memory and unswerving justice. Only much later in life did I realize he respected me as the clever child.

In a family of twelve you have to look after yourself pretty much without expecting too close an interest from a parent who is out working the farm from dawn to twilight. I believe he saw in me the one among his offspring who would later sum him up and possibly weigh him in the balance. This counted. He wasn't going to give me any quarter and he felt my mother's marginal indulgences should be rectified, but he nonetheless granted me some power of the future which he did not see in the others.

I suppose it was Jerry who drove me to music and

intellectual attainments. Jerry, the next brother below
and two years my junior, had our father's build. At
Cuttajo agricultural show in 1892, when he went in for
the contest of strength against grown men, local farmers
and fishermen from the fleet, he took out the cabbages
which were the third prize. He was just fourteen, that's
how I remember the date. Long before then he had outgrown me. So I was more or less driven, you could say, to
be the intellectual. I did my share of work and reckoned
on being pretty healthy. But you know how brothers are,
forever competing; they grow by beating each other
down. And Daniel, a year older than me, always disdained
young Jeremiah's company. Go and pester Pat, he'd say.
Always Pat. Danny was generally safe from me too because, although we're much the same build, that year difference gave him the edge. He saw himself as having a
destiny outside the family, Danny did. And though he
didn't want to go, when Pa sent him out into the world,
he told me later he was never happy before he succeeded
in getting away. That's how he saw it.

Michael still had the marks on his wrists at the time of the murder. Our policeman said this was where the killer had strapped them behind his back, as they were when his body was found. But I knew chain marks when I saw them. Pa had chained him to the bed-end the day before, to stop him playing up, drunk on Christmas cheer. Michael sometimes got chained without being drunk, just to keep him from behaving wildly. If you ask me, Pa felt good about being able to pin his twenty-nine-year-old son and get the locks on him though he lashed and punched and struggled to break free.

I meant to find out from Michael why he never tried escaping this humiliation. He was so cheerful and full of life, you see, besides being the most handsome man in the shire and all the girls crazy for him. Something held him. Something stronger than the disgrace of beatings long after he had grown beyond boyhood.

The time has come to introduce the third victim.

I think of Ellie standing on one leg at the stove, the free foot rubbing the back of her supporting knee while she stirred our breakfast porridge to keep it from burning, this being one of her jobs. We all took an interest because there's nothing so foul as burnt porridge; milk porridge, that is. We enjoyed the luxury of milk, thanks to our house cows. Ellie was independent. She thought for herself, she spoke up, she risked beatings (which she rarely got, in fact). She was the only person I ever met in all my life who could not tell the difference between good and evil.

I had already begun work at the convent while Ellen still attended classes there. "You look after your sister now, Mr Murphy," Sister Veronica would say to me when I came with the trap to take the young ones home. "She's as good as an angel." But Sister did not mean Katie, who *was* good as an angel, she meant Ellie.

I knew the truth. So did we all, Ellen included. Nothing was hidden from her. She wasn't in the slightest degree ashamed.

These three set out for the Boxing Day dance at Cuttajo: Michael still in the spring of life at twenty-nine; the eighteen-year-old Ellen, whom Sister Veronica mistook for an angel; and the most loving, most understanding, most beautiful of women, Norah, who never lived to celebrate her twenty-eighth birthday. They were the ones who did not come home by one o'clock in the morning, when Mum grew tired and lugged her duty into the bedroom where Pa snored, drunk on the store of liquor he had confiscated from Michael during the preceding weeks. They were the ones Billy McNeil the butcher went in search of at eight o'clock the next morning, 27th December 1898. Strange how persistent the number 8 becomes in all this: symbol of the knot and of the infinite.

The crown magistrate asked how McNeil knew where to go to find the bodies, since—in the words of one witness—they "lay a good mile off the road in their blood, hands strapped behind backs and the leaves above them sighing," also—by his own account—in "such a quiet spot a couple of tree trunks rubbing together in the wind gave me a shock, because the eerie moan seemed to come from the horse sprawled nearby with its legs out of kilter." McNeil replied that he had harnessed a gelding (one of ours, because the one he had brought to our house was by now the grieving carcase) and ridden towards Cuttajo, looking in every direction as he went. A bushman knows to watch for signs, even when he's just on his way somewhere to buy seed or woo a lady. Well, he did see a sign. Eight miles from Paradise he spotted wheel tracks heading off through the sliprail gate to the east, down towards the sea through that big paddock the Earnshaw family leave fallow every third year. He knew what he had found because one wheel was wobbly. From this he recognized his own sulky, the one Pa gave him at the wedding for taking Polly and her gossip off our hands.

Let me tell you, there's something in us we don't put a name to. We feel it, right enough, but can't say exactly what it is. Norah claimed to know that this was God, waiting for us to be worthy of Him who is already in us, hoping to shine out from what we do. Many's the time we talked it over. But I couldn't be brought to see life that way. If I could, I'd have taken up the offer to study for a priest. With Mum, she wore this mystery outside, enveloping her thick as a cape. With me, it has been a sensation of greatness; not a greatness belonging to God, but some power in my own body waiting for the chance to show.

With Michael it was a little thing, simply calling him home. He told me, because he was another one you could ask. Ellie laughed like rusty iron when I put the question to her. Young as she was and with her throat so slim and tender, she sounded older than the rest of us put together. "Is it what William lost?" she taunted me. "Is that what Pa knocked out of him?" To which Norah replied, "I want you to keep a respectful tongue in your head when you speak of your brother." But Ellie laughed more wildly, till we all ended up laughing.

Michael could never seem to really like her; Ellie, that is. As he was such an easygoing bloke, this surprised me. In certain ways they were alike, forever prancing around. And look at how soon he could recover from the beatings he suffered. She hardly ever got beaten, but if she had I don't think she would have cared. Just the opposite of Norah. Norah had feelings. Even the decision to go to the dance in the first place was a case of Norah thinking of others. There had been quite a stir earlier in the afternoon.

The whole family including Polly and her Bill drove down for the Yandilli Races seven miles south on a pretty rough road. Two sulkies went (one being McNeil's, which developed that wobble on the way in spite of the butcher saying he had fixed it for good) plus some of us riding: William, Michael, Jerry, and me. We planned a bit of a race along the straight. For the fun of the thing we swapped horses. Then the nag Jerry was on (mine) got a painful stone in her hoof. She might have gone lame, so he had to walk her till a cart came along, and beg a ride, tying the horse on behind; by his good luck this turned out to be Father Meaghan, a new priest in the district who was still falling over himself to win us locals over, though he never would succeed, being, as Pa said, wetter than a dish rag. Already he had put himself in bad with most folks by criticizing Father Gwilym's violin band. He had no time for godless entertainments, he declared in an accent freshly starched and ironed in Kilkenny. Did we have a gutful of Kilkenny before he had been among us a month! Anyhow, I'm wandering from the point. He it was who took Jeremiah along, Jerry sitting up there, bouncing gloomily because he was a habitual misery, and the mare he had been riding hopping now and again to nurse her tender foot. He must have been imagining what chance there was that Pa might come belting along in our big trap, full of fire, a silent reproachful Mum beside him, bearing down on this evidence of folly and the chance of losing a sound beast he could ill afford.

We three did not stick around to see.

William wouldn't even stop. He took one look at Jeremiah and dug his ankles in, hustling the little bay to get a safe distance ahead. I'd hung back as Michael offered to wait with him. But Jerry said in that fatalistic way: "What the hell, there's plenty of folks on the road today." We knew he wouldn't wait for long because we had already passed half a dozen parties which were not far behind. It was just a question of who happened by first. This was the end of our fooling. But of course, when we got there, Michael entered the races themselves. You could never hold him back. A bit of a lair, Michael. He swept his hat off to this one and that and smiled for all the ladies whether he knew them or not, while young Johnnie and his mates killed themselves laughing at him. Though what with the times Michael had been to Yandilli and to the bigger town of Bunda beyond, these females mostly did know him, at least by sight.

But I was telling you about Ellie, wasn't I? Yes, and how Michael never seemed to like her. This day at the races, while we were eating our picnic, just our family minus Polly who went to her Billy's family picnic (and for half an hour she and Billy and Billy's old folks came visiting us), Ellie asked who was going to the Cuttajo dance, because we'd all been discussing it for a fortnight at least but nobody could seem to arrive at a decision. "Michael?" she said straight off as if he was the one she had most in mind, "are you on my side?" And he shied off. So cheerful he had been till then. He grew suddenly glum as Jeremiah and wanted to know why him? Well, Norah came right out and ticked him off for trying to cool the girl's enthusiasm and treating her like a child still.

I don't remember when he changed his mind and started saying he was definitely going. I suspect I was the one who began it anyhow by whingeing about being expected at work when I'd far rather have a pretty sister invite me to the dance than an ugly Sister boss me around at the convent, plus having to clear the rubbish out of the scullery, which was always my first job and the one I hated most. Pa rumbled and swung a punch at my head from where he sat on the grass, a halfhearted effort which missed. He said he wouldn't hear indecencies from whelps. Mum leaned over to push me against a nearby tree. That awful hot deadweight of her. But she kept her face turned away and stirred the dark around her with mutterings about blasphemy, not to mention honouring thy father and thy mother. I slipped out and ran off, laughing at them, mortified, yet confident I could get away with just about anything on Boxing Day, when so many neighbours gathered, all trying to outdo one another in respectability. Sure enough, the Willoughbys from Burnt

Ridge Road called across to us: "You've got a bright
prospect there, Mrs Murphy!" Mum looked out at Belle
Willoughby through her cloud and nodded like the end
of the world. They thought this was meant to be a great
joke and everybody laughed successfully. Maybe it was.
With our mother you couldn't tell what she might intend.
While I was doing the rounds of people I knew, so as not
to have to go back to my place, Michael must have come
good with his promise to take Ellen dancing. But later
when we stopped on the road—I was going straight
through to work but I waited with the others while
Johnnie opened the gate to Paradise—and they confirmed their plan to have a bite to eat before setting out
for the evening's fun, Norah did let slip an expression
which took me by surprise. She said to Ellie: "I shall be
there to look after you."

As she said this, Jeremiah coughed loudly like the
stupid kid he was at heart, though only two days off
twenty. I have everything particularly clear in my
memory. "Hark at the frogs," Katie said. And truly, frogs
were singing out so loud you could think yourself deaf,
which wouldn't have been surprising if it was about to
rain, but it wasn't. Maybe they were singing in protest
against the driest Christmas on record. We always expected rain at that time of year. The races were usually
run in hot muddy conditions.

I don't doubt it was this dusty weather which put
everyone in such a wild mood, laughing like desperadoes

because what else could you do but go mad, seeing the grass parch and get kicked to powder while your beasts lost condition? Apart from growing wheat, we ran steers at the time, before William—with the farsightedness of the simple—converted the place to dairy cattle.

That Christmas night when Norah was dressing Michael's wound she let slip her indignation at Pa's cruelty. Jerry, who was there with us, spoke up harshly. "Cruel is not a word for Pa," he explained, "Pa has to be one step ahead. Look over there." He pointed to the open paddock in moonlight. "That was filled with enemies: trees, men, women, kangaroos. They had to be chopped down one by one to make room for us. The fences keep nothing out, they are just a sign that beyond this point any intruder has him to deal with." Norah asked: "Even death itself?" Jerry nodded and went on: "When Pa whips Mike, it's because he sees the enemy in him. His job is to keep us up to the mark. And if he thought you were against him, he just would not understand." I could see Norah's astonishment when, at this point, Michael agreed. Though perhaps he only did so because he was drunk, or perhaps for the sake of Christmas.

Anyway, the next night he was dead. Both he and Norah were dead. And Jeremiah knew he had said dangerous things in front of me, like Pa seeing the enemy in Michael, like Pa not understanding those of us who were against him, and this could only mean Norah our comforter. Or Ellie, the one neither like him (as Jerry was) nor afraid of him.

Our house had never been painted. The wood grew silver-grey, decorated with swirls of weatherworn grain. I think it never truly had an outside. The verandah all round (the style you still see in Queensland) made it like a house whose walls had been taken down, if you know what I mean. You looked straight in to the skeleton, among rooms and open doors, with, often enough, the family sprawled or squatting on the verandah in the spaces between the posts which held up its flimsy iron roof.

The house sat low. The soil lay flat around it, just two steps down, deep in dead dust for the dry half of the year and green during the wet. Of a morning in those half-seasons between, mist would drift indoors from the verandah, right to the most private rooms, and Mum's gloom would come sailing out, tearing this mist to frayed stuff as it clung round her; just the way sister Ellen might rush by in a swirl of white; or the frothy milk pinging into a pail, warmed by its own steaminess, would be almost invisible while damp air clung to the underside of our house cows.

That was my job, milking the cows before breakfast, with my hands chapped and unwilling and my mind too quilted by sleep for taking in the world of paddock and pens, the big spongy tufts of grass, or long slim branches of swamp mahoganies reaching up to catch handfuls of leaves from the sky.

I put things this way, let me confess, because I have had many more years for seeing what I used to miss. I am the one who still lives in the house. I am the chief one, at least. Jeremiah in his wheelchair shares it, also William. Willie's job is pulling down the holland blinds at night. Now we have a main road passing not a hundred yards from our door, we never can tell who might be snooping. He also catapults the blinds up again in the morning. If they won't snap quickly enough, he raises them twice. Their edges are cracked and torn along the sides from being worked too fast and crooked. He does the whole house, letting our warmth and darkness escape to run out all over the soil. The house is sometimes floating on water when the January rains are heavy and we old men, William and I and Mack, as we call Bill McNeil, who lives in the kennel at the back, have to paddle through it with trousers rolled up above the knee. Not Jerry, though. It would never do for his wheelchair to rust. He trundles round the place, wheels grinding and thundering over bare floorboards. At least he can never sneak up on you. But William is always doing that.

Willie knows he is simple. And because of this, I question whether he *can* be. He even knows how he first became simple, remembers the bashing Pa gave him, Pa who never laughed. He remembers because he is forever telling us the same tale in his droopy way: I was heading up north to find work on the railway, that's why he bashed the daylights out of me, he busted my ribs and my head. Other times Willie tries the alternative opening: Pa put these wasps in my head.

And he will thump one ear as if we might expect to see a buzzing swarm of anger come flying out the other.

We four are the ones who dare not die. Those murders keep us alive, William, Jeremiah, Mack, and me. We are strengthened by the knowledge that one of us has blood on his hands. Such is the true gold of the conscience: we are not kidding ourselves with little household slip-ups, nor petty confessions worth only a couple of Hail Marys.

And then there's Pa. He stays in the house with us too. Only you cannot rightly say he lives there, being dead this last forty-three years. He sits at the head of the table. It must be the anger that preserves him. He doesn't need to talk. Well, he seldom did talk much at the best of times. At least he keeps the flies off. They won't come near the place with him here. Something in nature, I dare say.

The women never understood silence, except Mum. And all that is left of her is a shadow which moves from one corner to another to another, under the table, behind the sideboard. She is always moving, though you might never catch her at it. Even if you look as hard as you please, she seems to stay stock-still, lying doggo, but an hour later, when you think of her again, she has gone, lurking now behind the door or at the side of her famous wood stove. She doesn't mind the heat. She doesn't mind the cold either. All she is shy of is light. So when Willie does his rounds, and he's pretty slow, being ninety-one, snapping up those blinds, he is not just letting the warmth out, he is shooting the house full of light, driving our mother frantic, so she vanishes from where she filled whole rooms and choked us with her solid old weight, to pop up here and there underneath lumps of furniture she once took such pride in. I cannot say I pity her; she has some answering to do, and the Good Lord will not be mocked.

Did I tell you that we all look alike? Not just the three brothers and father at present in our house being invaded by mist, but Mum and the other seven brothers and sisters as well. Our parents could have been identical twins, their likeness was so remarkable many people commented on it—sometimes, I suspect, to hint that there might be untold secrets. The real puzzle was this: though Norah was the most beautiful woman you could imagine, the youngest sister, Katie the clown, looked so ugly she made you laugh. They had the same nose, same mouth, same eyes and forehead, but the spaces were different. Where in Norah this added up to a face beautiful as an angel in the holy pictures Father Gwilym gave us for good behaviour, in Katie they seemed about to fall apart, constantly having to be screwed and twisted to keep them together; she knew she could not allow them to rest idle or her face might collapse. Now, why did I use a word like *collapse?* I don't know, but I can't think of any other way to give an impression of how sad her jokes were, how desperate she was to stay alive in spite of our mother and father. Mum would appear in a drift of mist, steering her darkness before her, ready to stifle the least sign of joy in the family short of godlessness or cruelty; Pa, just behind her, knew nothing other than cruelty in his powerful ignorance. Some of us ducked for cover or rushed off to our chores, William cringing into his stupid state of a blank mind; others like Michael, who never learnt, habitually greeted them openly; and the two little ones, Johnnie and Kate, were just as likely to begin horsing around and getting in everyone's way. Strange, that. Only Jerry stayed late in bed. In Jerry they found their match, a giant like themselves. If it comes to the point, I suppose you could say he was the one they had waited for.

We don't know exactly when Pa died. He was getting old. He always sat in that carver chair, and one day in 1913 we realized we had not seen him out of it for about a month. He could have chosen any moment during this period to go. But his rage lived on in the way he sat.

People had come in and gone out—including a police-man checking on a chicken theft—nodded and greeted him, and left without noticing any change. I think he felt cheated by those murders, that was it. Michael he despised, and only the day before the tragedy, after eating Christmas dinner, Pa had wrestled him to the floor and chained him on a bed-end; Norah he hated because she kept us human, undoing all the work he and Mum put in to have us beasts for life (obedient for life, as they would term it); but I think he was a little unnerved by Ellen, she didn't react against him like the younger ones who clowned and joked their way out of the nightmare, she didn't care; she was the only one apart from Jeremiah not afraid of him. But she was more of a puzzle than Jerry, who, at least in temperament, sided with him. She never considered Pa cruel, accepting the way he showed himself to be. He couldn't fathom that, if you ask me, and wasn't com-fortable with it either. So—since I do not believe he felt any particular shock or bereavement, nor even outrage at the crime—I can only explain it as the idea that some-body had stolen from him what he didn't expect ever to have stolen: his power. By these three, more than any others among us, he set the boundaries of his power. In all he thought of them when they were alive, he never once guarded against seeing them dead. His rage prejudiced the opinion of at least some members of the police commission at the magisterial enquiry. Yes, there was an enquiry, conducted by Mr A. H. Warner Shand,

Acting Police Magistrate at Nowra, plus the Commissioner of Police, an inspector and two sub-inspectors. The enquiry lasted thirteen sitting days, during which forty-five witnesses were examined. None of the others suffered such persistent hounding as Pa. Plainly the magistrate thought he might uncover enough evidence to commit Pa for trial. The deposition clerk wrote eight hundred and thirty-five pages of depositions. It came to nothing.

I ought to tell you about Billy McNeil, the butcher Polly married in one of her fits of silliness. Mack, as we call him, is one of those fellows who thinks it is okay to repeat to you what you have already said to him. "This rain is set in for a week," you might offer as a greeting. To which he'd reply, after taking a few moments' silence: "Set in for about a week, I shouldn't be surprised." He was the one to nearly drive the magistrate mad. You may imagine: "If your memory is so accurate, Mr McNeil, concerning how you first found the victims' bodies, might you, perhaps, care to explain how it was that you forgot your own brother-in-law's name a moment ago and referred to him as Patrick and not Michael?" "Well," he answered solemn and important, "I forgot and called him Patrick and not Michael. When," he added apologetically, "it was Michael."

Young Johnnie, waiting his turn in the public gallery, as we called the bench at the back of our courthouse, laughed loud as a goat gone crazy. The town was scandalized.

The paddock where they lay violated and shot, two of them together and Norah separate at the foot of a spotted-gum, stood quiet with that buzzing muffled hush of something you will never forget . . . thick from the horror that had been there, frogs dumb for a whole day after the shock of a lifetime. Imagine it as if the boulder had been rolled from the mouth of Nicodemus's cave to show, instead of the Living Dead offering words of comfort, the dead alive with a million flies, faces and wounds seething black wings and legs. Blowflies crawled and clustered up the girls' skirts and fought for the best portion of their thighs.

Mack found the victims at 8.30 a.m. According to him he rode straight to Cuttajo and made enquiries for Sergeant Arrell at the Brian Boru Hotel, where they directed him down the street to the fishing wharf. There he told the sergeant his story at 9.15 a.m. It was 27th December. Christmas dinner had weighed on the stomach for only a day and a half, and our winnings from the Yandilli races still jingled in our pockets. You may be sure we did win too. Luck of the Irish. We won every year. Maybe only a few shillings, but we always came out in front. Clem Brewster, who acted as bookmaker once he'd closed his mercery store for the holiday, used to smack his forehead and groan: "Here come the bloody Murphys to clean me out of my honest earnings!"

Sergeant Arrell remained a decent-enough cove, as police drunks go, till he got scared of growing old and turned vicious. At the time I'm speaking of he was still

only about forty-five, though. He rode back with McNeil
and reported what he saw:

I found the bodies of Michael Murphy and Ellen Murphy
lying back to back, quite close one to the other. Twelve feet
from the man's head lay a heavy bludgeon-stick. I observed
blood and brains stuck to the thick end of this weapon. The
brains I surmised to come from Ellen, whose head was seriously smashed and the brains falling out of the back of the
skull. Michael's skull was also smashed on the right-hand side.
The body of the woman Norah Murphy lay somewhat apart.
Also her head had been smashed, presumably with the identical
weapon, this time on the left side of the skull. Signs of dishev-
elment suggested they had been violated and had struggled
for their honour as well as their lives. Both also had their hands
and feet tied. Norah, the one laying apart from the others, also
had a leather hame strap fastened tight around her neck. The
sulky stood a few yards off with a dead horse still in the shafts,
its reins had been carried forward and looped over the bit. The
beast lay on the right-hand shaft, which had not broken, there
was a bullet hole in its head, point-blank.

Note: The post-mortem examination confirmed that the
women had indeed been violated, besides discovering that
Michael Murphy was shot in addition to being battered, a bullet
lodged in his brain.

When we came to see the bodies and knelt down to check
that they were dead, flies arose as a swarm. The most awful thing was to see how beautiful the flies appeared at
this moment—no longer black but luminous in the tilt-
ing light.

We stood back to allow Mum her rights as principal

mourner. Even Pa recognized that death, like birth, is women's business and shows the men's business of labour and war as shallow by comparison. But our mother, pushing her fate across rough turf and finding it heavy to move as a barrow full of dirt, stood back still. When the flies settled again, the loudest noise was Mum's breathing. At last she spoke, without any show of surprise or tears: "Now I have got only seven." And there we all were, though she did not check. Pa never went near, he took root like another old tree and let the breeze sort among the hairs of his beard, bringing out the white ones more clearly than they had ever seemed before. You wouldn't catch white hairs on Mum; not till her dying day did she have one—black was her colour, and so she stayed. She didn't need to change clothes for mourning, she already wore mourning as her everyday. She didn't even need to change expression. She made no move towards death, and when it came rushing at her she was not a bit surprised.

Mum died only four months later, at the age of fifty-five. The smell of our house changed once she was gone, so that we knew then for the first time that it was a smell Mum created. I have only caught a whiff of anything like it a few times in the years since; and each time I have found myself carried straight back to the way things were, the dim pictures of our grandparents reflecting her walking past as a dusking of wind across water, the floorboards and wall studs creaking an accompaniment to every move, big body stirring her special brew of air. I suppose this brew consisted of lingering aromas from the food she cooked, wild herbs she dried to slip among the linen, goanna oil which she massaged into her scalp to prevent her hair going thin, miscellaneous odours of our coming and goings (including even accidents)—all were breathed in by her, mixed and breathed out in immense lungfuls of her own unique blend. She only ever went outdoors to go to the privy or mass, or to do the washing and hang it up, yet she breathed a tender air of bread and old clover. As a result the place became unlike anyone else's house. To me, the word *home* calls to mind this smell more than anything else.

During our last half century it has been lost.

Danny's wife screamed. Did I tell you she was staying with us over Christmas too? Yes, Danny's wife and Polly's husband. They were the only two to be married into the family at that stage. Although our young ones, Kate and Johnnie, got spliced later on, four out of ten isn't many. And curiously, not one of them had a child survive. It was said that Johnnie risked damnation with his contraceptives, but I don't know. Polly gave birth to twins, both stillborn. Kate herself died in labour and her son Paul, who was the only living nephew I ever knew, lasted till he was three. So the line will die out when my brothers and I finally earn our release.

Well, as I say, Danny's wife screamed. Remember, we were still at the site of the murders. The sound of it went nowhere, the bush just gulped it in and she was left, mouth open, appearing foolish. Beryl, her name was, which Mum declared couldn't be Christian at all. The explanation had to rest with the fact that Beryl was bred a Protestant and converted only when she came to marry Dan. Perhaps this was to prove how much she loved him, though by then he'd already become a policeman and it's a specimen of freakishness in a woman to love a policeman. Poor lass was probably on edge anyway, Mum having given notice that she would not stand for any hanky-panky in her house at night.

When Danny's wife or Polly's husband came to visit they bunked in with us, put to bed in the boys' rooms or the girls' room, as the case might be. Also, this Beryl claimed she had had inklings. You see, on that Boxing Day, policeman Danny got up first in the morning (usually it was me for my milking stint, but I felt dog-tired) and realized the sulky had not been put back in the yard. He went to the room which Beryl shared with Norah and Ellen. He found his wife alone. The other beds hadn't been slept in. Then they woke Mack McNeil because the sulky was his now, and at this stage the worst thing likely would have been a breakdown or else that one wheel finally come adrift.

If you ask me, Beryl looked like a pig when she screamed, nostrils wide and square face all chops and chaps. She stayed this way. Right till her end in 1938, the scream stuck on her face.

Barney Barnett had not been invited for Christmas because he wasn't one of the family. Since he was only a fiancé and destined never to get any closer, our parents were unlikely to clutter their house with the likes of him when it was already so crowded we fell over one another and cursing could more often be heard than celebrating. He did join our picnic at the race meeting, however. Also he challenged Michael in the fifth event, the eight furlongs, run immediately after lunch. He never liked Michael, to express it mildly, and took any opportunity of trying to put him down or make him appear stupid. Come to think of it, he behaved as if Michael was a rival for Ellie's admiration: little did he know they avoided one another at home. Or perhaps he was truly infatuated and had the insight of love. The family did not bother to include Barney among the mourners. Pa said the fellow could read all he needed to know in the newspaper.

The Bunda *Advocate* made a meal of it on 29th December. The editor recognized the only chance of glory ever likely to fall into his lap.

MURDER.

———

At Cuttajo on Boxing Night

———

One of the murders of the Century

———

The Worst in Australia

———

Two Sisters
Ravished and Mur-
dered

———

Their Brother Also
Killed

———

A Fiendish Crime

———

A Terrible Story

———

Full Details

———

When we were dressed for the funeral, Barney Barnett
came riding up to the house. He simply slung the reins
over the piebald's head and left her there to graze on a
patch of cloud. We had never seen such a thing. He came
wading through the prohibitions, up our two steps,
among unmade beds on the verandah, and into the big
room with Pa sitting where he is now in a carver chair
at the head of the table. Here Barney lifted his rifle and
fired a single shot, apparently aimed to kill. The statement of a man who passes his own judgment. He came
and he acted: nothing like the sly coquettish confession
he later offered the police inspector from Sydney. But
the joke was that he missed. Even at point-blank range
he couldn't hit a giant like Pa. You'd wonder how he ever

shot any game or caught a feed for his table. You certainly wondered how he expected to support our sister. Pa never moved, but he did speak. He said: "If you come in reach of these hands, son, I'll choke the life out of you, and that's a promise."

So Barney fled. He rode away without shutting any gates. Danny's opinion at the time was that if he had killed Pa this would have been the first life he had taken, barring our pig . . . It was the opinion he repeated, as a police constable on oath, in the courthouse. Ellen, he said, had escaped marrying a cove yellower than his teeth.

When I think of Barney lying in bed, no more than four miles from our place, hanging on by a single finger, crows fluttering in his scavenger eyes, I want to choke him myself. Him! Where did he get the idea he could just pick and choose his time or that he was big enough for fame? Dismal all his life. What price had he paid to expect anything more than a dismal death? Drunk with pride that he scored an inspector instead of Frank, our local cop, he was too flushed from hopes of a second chance at life to notice a twist in the police inspector's question: "Why did you do that, Mr Barnett?"

What was the meaning: Why did he bash the horse's brains out, or why did he use the bludgeon-stick, or why did he concoct a confession? He had probably rehearsed this scene a thousand times, over the years, till the lines came to be the most real thing in his life, a reality all by themselves and nothing to do with what happened. The priest gave him absolution and he reckoned he would make it into the annals of notorious crime, his name to live forever, glorified by the murder of the century.

But this inspector knew that a murderer wasn't one to forget what he had done, wasn't one to say he bashed the horse's brains out with a bludgeon-stick (Sergeant Arrell's word, anyway) when the horse was shot. Also, both those shots in the head, the one in the horse's and the other in Michael's, were perfect shots. Whereas the bullet Barney aimed at my father, sitting in all his broadness and never flinching, is bedded in our wall at home a good arm's length wide of where Pa still sits as a witness.

I am beyond that age when a man's mind occasionally tumbles headlong down shafts of memory, glimpsing some small moment among humble objects and feeling his heart contract with grief for a life he once led: I have reached the point where this is my *normal* condition. Now and then the reverse happens and I am swept up level with the present, dumped in my shell somewhere I'd rather not be, longing only to sink back to a region offering room for hope, time for seeing every least thing as completely as human eyes can see.

This is why I found Barney Barnett so hard to get along with. He saw the past just the way he had when fifty, or thirty-five, or twenty-eight. He didn't acquire the gift of wisdom, having never made the past his own. He still lived it among strangers, kidding himself till the end that he had a choice open to him.

The confession killed him. He suffered a seizure right there, with us watching. The priest mumbled devout sentiments, Pa's stallion let drop a couple of extra globes, and the inspector snapped his briefcase shut, not troubling to disguise his irritation.

Hateful as Barnett was, I couldn't leave his finger caught like a baby's. I pulled it out from where he had hooked it through his grandma's lace border. The priest poked at the dead eyelids with a shrinking gesture, needing several attempts to close the eyes. Afterwards, two little rimples of skin smoothed themselves, settling to the shape of the eyeball so you would swear, for an instant, that he was cheating us still.

Good luck to you, Barney! I thought. You took the plunge in the end, you rat. Even though it failed, this was better than nothing.

Outside in the yard the inspector's car door shut. After a pause the motor roared to life, gunning away through the gate. We said nothing: Willie, Jeremiah, Mack, and me. Pa's horse shifted its weight from one haunch to the other: his hat rose an inch to touch the ceiling and then sank again.

Moments later, a fine pall of dust drifted in through the open window to settle over the bed and the face of the poor failure in it.

My mother's one fancy was a bead curtain. This hung across the doorway between the livingroom and a small workroom where she sewed and knitted and slammed flat-irons along yards of bulky skirts, breathing a tart stench of hot cloth and raw soap and giving it out, even this, as her musty-green smell of home. The workroom had better light than any other part of the house. In the middle of the inner wall, fringes of this light hung as drops, trapped by the beads—red light, sapphire light, and drops of clear water.

Norah, learning the finer points of housekeeping from her, often worked there too. At these times, I would stand long minutes in the livingroom looking out through that glittering waterfall at the younger woman's bent head, at tender stray hairs on her nape as she stitched some cloth deftly and sang to herself, not at all suppressed by any mushrooming resentful secrecy. Mum, knowing the load of mending still waited in her basket, would let the job manage itself while she withdrew further into an obscurity of intentions.

Perhaps what the old lady liked about that bead curtain was the warning it gave when anyone came through, clittering and shivering jewelled light. Sometimes she might sense me there and shoot a hot look into the gloom, straining to see past her own bright innovation. Once or twice she caught me and called: Is there no work left round the farm? Or: Idle hands are the Devil's holiday. Or she'd thrust a handful of repaired socks towards me and say: Put these in Willie's cupboard on your way to the paddock.

She knew why I was there. And I knew she knew. Part of her fate was the slow plan shaping; she had changed her mind. To save me, she needed to get me out of the house and keep me out of it. The chief obstacle was that I had always been her favourite. She knew I had to be expelled, but she wanted me to stay. And her heart prevailed. She bullied me and crushed me and rolled her scorn over any small thing I did, in order to stifle my spirit. She refused to treat me as a man and called me Boy right till she died. All because I was the one she longed to keep, I know it. She hungered for me to remain a child and dependent. Just like Pa beat Willie into an idiot because he couldn't bear the idea of living without him, so she loved me and called me Boy. There we were, Willie and I . . . the two they loved.

They respected Jeremiah for being one of their kind

and an equal, but this is not to imply any actual warmth towards him. Each male child was welcomed as an investment, a free labourer. They never loved the girls at all, as a general rule. Despite the way Mum made a bit of an exception of Polly, Pa couldn't see the back of the goose fast enough; also they got rid of Danny, though he hung about and trailed after Pa with worship in his cow eyes. That was the way they rewarded the ones they chose as breeding stock for the family's future. But how were they to see any value in generosity, as such, the quality both Norah and Michael had? Quite separate was the indifference with which they treated young John and Kate, whom they ignored as they might ignore a couple of boisterous puppies our blue-heeler bitch had unfortunately whelped. The only one they were afraid of was Ellen, because they knew she thought them no different from other people. Oh yes, her look would say while Pa dragged Michael lashing and kicking into his bedroom, throwing him bodily against the walls and chaining him up for a night, the victim bellowing and swearing, oh yes, well, this is one of the ways the human animal is in the habit of behaving.

So when Pa stormed back to finish dinner and struck out with his huge paw to knock Michael's rum bottle on the floor where Norah would have to clean up the shattered glass, still glorying in his mastery, growing more a giant than ever and Mum a giantess because of him, the only eyes he would not meet were Ellen's. Ellen gazing cool and, you might say, scientific. That was it: she examined our parents as specimens she might one day find a use for. Her hands were transparent from churning butter, this being her job as mine was milking. She skimmed the cream and poured it into the churn's tray, turning the handle and watching a whole series of ribbed wooden rollers thresh the cream. Unlike me, she loved her job. Having slapped the pats between oblong oak spatulas to shape them ready for storing in the drip-cooler, she pressed a carved seal on the top, printing a four-leaf clover, which was the family sign. All our lives butter would be stamped with that four-leaf clover, ever more steadily once Ellie was old enough to take charge of this refinement. Her transparent hands stayed clenched in death, as we saw when we arrived at the scene of murder—the opposite of Norah's, which spread open and helpless under swooning flies.

Another reason for Pa not making any move to crush Ellen like he crushed the older ones among us was that he saw she made his litter more complete. She gave him something to marvel at. Because she made no distinction between right and wrong, he could not guess how he figured in her judgment. When he laid Willie out at a blow, or Michael or me for that matter, he could tell we hated him, and accepted our hating as a measure of his strength. This made him feel good, if anything ever did. He knew too that, as he stood over the fallen body, Norah would be waiting her chance to move in with a cool clean cloth and gentle fingers, with healing words whose calm grew deeper the more barbaric his outburst; this was a measure of himself as well. Even with the young ones when they learned to laugh, transforming pain and fear to clowning, he could see through their antics and discover himself clear behind them. But Ellen had him baffled. I think he believed that given long enough he would come to see into her too, and that then he could draw forth a new treasure for his collection of beasts.

All this while, you could say, we grew closer. Except three: Jerry single as an alien, Willie too far gone to be any use in the survival game, and Polly, whose refuge of silliness was entirely selfish. The rest among us found our world complete. I suppose we loved one another.

I once tried to get Norah a husband. A mate of mine I'd known from school had a brother Norah's age. I was seventeen at the time and this bloke Artie Earnshaw was twenty-three, just right, a year older than Norah. He was a local champion, you could say. He swam and chopped wood faster than any man his age in the shire; though a bit heavy for riding, he stood undefeated in the Bunda agricultural show boxing carnival. And I knew him. I went out to get him for Norah. I put myself in his way. I borrowed his tools (but not his axe, which he would never lend) and returned them unused, cleaner than ever, plus a bag of mushrooms picked one morning and taken up to the gate when I knew he'd be passing on his way to work the day the forestry teams felled a patch of timber between us and Cuttajo. I risked being skinned alive by Pa, wasting a whole half hour waiting for him to come by, and then I was almost too shocked to speak.

What could I say? It looked wrong for me to pick mushrooms for him. He might take it amiss and beat me up on the spot, so I came to the point and lied. I told him they were a present (what inspiration) from my sister Norah. So the lie hovered between us.

Artie Earnshaw paid her a visit and, from what I saw and overheard, was fascinated by her. The fascination deepened when she insisted she had sent him nothing. Probably he disbelieved her, recognizing this as a symptom of modesty. They might have gone on to make a couple, except that I suddenly realized what he meant by his attentions, that he looked on her as flesh to be possessed, that she could become wholly his, and I had behaved like a complete idiot in not facing the fact. I wanted to kill Artie as he stood easy on the verandah, leaning back on his hips, broad hands making simple gestures of being pleased, his worn boots of an active man, and his throaty musical laugh. She fancied him. This wound now worked its pain so deeply in me I could not remember how I had felt before. He said he might call again. But I swore he would not win her off me so easily, because my claims on her had been precious long before we ever heard of him.

I strolled out of my room and through the kitchen to the top of the two steps. We were close enough for us to have shaken hands. I saw then that our family had a destiny and would be truly doomed if we fought against it. I heard my voice break free from shyness (we were all shy except Ellen): "I've got to own up," my voice said, so that it became the voice of the space still between them, that space ripe with afternoon sunshine, polished to the roundness of full golden fruit. "It was a joke, Artie." I glanced at Norah and then away, horrified by the instant flame of hatred in her eyes, fearing this far more than any violence he could do to me. I hung my head and confessed: "I didn't mean it, Norah, I didn't think anything would happen. They were good mushrooms," I added lamely, already throbbing with triumph at having reached her deeply.

Artie Earnshaw stared at me, stared as a man will who is caught on a razor-edge and undecided whether to hit out to restore his pride or draw the clown by the shoulder, holding him close as much as to say: Look, what you thought of as a prank is something we shall all live to thank you for throughout the rest of our lives. And Norah was keeping him on that razor-edge. By her silence, by the stricken whiteness of her anger and the flush of blood following it, she held him back, forbade him either action, and demolished his pride as anything worth restoring in this case. I know, because I mustered the courage to turn my appeal to her again.

Norah's wonderful slow smile gathered and blossomed. This was not a smile for Artie, generous enough for me also to find forgiveness in it, but the other way round. She kept him in suspense as she spoke exclusively to me: "Then, Pat, you have put your sister in an unpardonable position with Mr Earnshaw," she said.

He knew this cut him out altogether. He wasn't even

to be permitted the right to thump me as I deserved. He
was not permitted feelings at all. He was to become,
solely, the person to whom she offered her gift of gratitude. Gratitude was what he must make do with. Nothing of the flesh, nor anything of the spirit would be his
now. He had given her . . . me.

I saw him often since. He lived to a good age, being
happy with the wife he did marry and his six children. It
was in Earnshaw's paddock, about a mile and a half from
his house, which was still his father's house then, that
Norah was murdered. Artie, as one of the witnesses at
the magisterial enquiry, said he could not understand
why we Murphys appeared so unmoved by the crime. At
the time, his father had sent him on their best roan
gelding to carry the news from Mack and Sergeant
Arrell to our place. He set off, by then a young married
man, just twenty-eight and with two fine daughters, filled
with the shock of what he had seen. And filled with dread
at having to break such news to a family he had once been
as friendly towards as any man could claim.

I remember him riding up, face bright red with hectic
news and the wild gallop, strong hands clenching on air
as he greeted me, asking whether my ma and pa were
home because he wished to have a private word with
them. As he later told the court, once indoors he found
himself facing both parents, the mother towering over
even him (he was a man six foot tall) and the father
sitting at a table, both dark in the dim room. The kindest
thing he could think of was to tell them bluntly that there

had been a murder, or three murders. By this time, I should mention, I was an unseen witness and I heard him, in his manly way, bring it all out—clear, simple, yet made gentle by his feelings on their behalf. I stayed on the other side of that bead curtain in Mum's workroom.

Silence.

"I know this is a terrible shock," he added. "Will you come back with me now?"

"No. We'll finish the chores and then we'll come," Pa said.

Artie knew his duty and wasn't the type to back down.

"The police sergeant is waiting; nothing can be done till you show up."

"Do you hear me?" Pa thundered quietly. "We'll come when we're ready. All dead you say?" he asked a moment later as Artie reached the door.

"Yes." And you could hear from his tone he thought this was a breakthrough to a more natural turn.

But Pa simply left it at that; and Mum wheeled her weight of air around, droving it out into the scullery without a single word, without a cry or a tear, without even seeming interested.

Speaking personally, I have a notion that Artie Earnshaw still felt a soft spot for our Norah. He was more shaken by seeing her corpse than he'd admit.

Mum's task was to bully the youngsters. They, of course, though supposed to be washing the dishes, hung suspended in a stone-cold hush, striving to suppress the blood's clamour and overhear what our handsome neigh-

bour came to say. This is what I surmise because, from
where I stood in the workroom, I heard a sudden banging
of pots, scuffles, and a stifled shriek. At that moment a
thought arrived in my mind which has never left it
since: Mum behaves like a woman who is barren.

True; her ample body, her outsized breasts and hips
were more for armoured padding than child-succouring
or child-bearing. Then I was visited by the further idea
of Pa being much the same, giant though he was. His
potency had never been of a giving kind. Yet they were
fertile, as the ten of us attested. They must be victims:
this was the conclusion I reached. They must be victims of
an unwanted, unnatural fertility, hating us for coming. I
imagined their coupling as stubborn and sullen. Often
enough we heard the mountainous shudders of it throughout the night, but I recognized it now, not as consumma-
tion or joy, but as a despairing admission that the flesh
is doomed.

In fairness, I ought to explain that I myself have only
ever once made love to a woman. The power in me then
was beyond anything I thought possible of the human
body—and her fierceness, for a gentle woman, so . . .
ravenous, I have never brought myself to the test again.
Or, put it this way, as we lay burning together, I thought
of my parents, fearing maybe they too had felt this divine
fury the first time, lost in each other just that once and
never finding their way out of the labyrinth again (Father
Gwilym had told me the story of Orpheus and Eurydice)

—certainly past the need of talking as they trod through hell. Might it be that they looked back, though forbidden to live the same experience twice, and sank into an underworld of failure each time they were within reach of rising to a new and saving moment? And the failures swelling her womb, hard as knotted rope? I recognized, in myself and my brothers and sisters, the mockery of their fumbled attempts to find freedom once more. I saw their fertility as something separate, malignant, and coarse.

The larder and scullery retained the same coolness. They shared a single doorway. They had been built from stone as a separate structure linked to the kitchen. The only other solid parts of our house were two brick chimneys: one stood outside the kitchen wall to carry smoke from the stove recess, while the other, the taller one, leaned against the front of the house, a verandah roof wrapping around it, for the fire in our main room. Mum lived in her larder because she liked its raw air in all weathers, plus the smell of grain, the cold sweet meat under wire covers, and aromatic stores like tea. Back in the scullery she could slap my sisters with her open hand and then in the larder be alone with her satisfaction afterwards, because no one but her was ever allowed there. Unless it was the Polly of old, helping bring out ingredients for our Christmas puddings and dumping them on the kitchen table ready to be mixed.

When Artie Earnshaw left, Mum, having said not a

word to her husband, stood long minutes in the cold larder surrounded by shelves of dead meat, dried fruit, and crushed seeds.

One thing more than anything else persuades me I was right. Jeremiah. They were always at peace with Jeremiah. My idea is that he had the proper gloom, the same shape and ponderousness as their own failure. He did not behave as a child of fertility, he never laughed or ran amok. He offered them a mirror for the lumps of un-willing flesh they had become. When I was attending special lessons with the priest and being taught to enter the world of Raphael and Swift, Father Gwilym once placed his cool hand on my knee and said: "I believe I shall never break through the boy's shell." I knew who he meant. And a moment later, when he had withdrawn his hand, leaving a colder impression of it still there, he added: "It is as if all his growing up were done before he had the chance to be a child."

My guess is that Jerry has remained virgin to this day. Now he is seventy-eight and crippled, he doesn't have much time for cutting loose, either.

It is possible our parents had the idea that if we could only fight back we might drive them out of their morbid tomb and, vulnerably, into each other's arms again with a young passion. Likewise, Ellen's perversity, as I think about it, possibly gave them promise of challenges they had not foreseen. Did her lack of morality, her inability to judge them cruel, set lust flickering, warning symptoms of a terrible eruption doomed to growl down and hibernate under the shelter of violence or indifference? So Willie's idiocy, Polly's silliness, Michael's gaiety, Norah's warmth, Daniel's earnestness, and the young ones' clowning . . . all were monstrous growths of their search to find again that Eden of the sexual act stumbled upon in innocence.

They went to mass because they had it in for God.

I want to show you what we were like in the light of love. You could easily imagine us (in love) as a family of pigs, thick with bristly skin and hard round meat, bouncing off each other if we collided, our short thick legs and knobbly knees, our eyes of the captured always on the lookout for a hole in the fence, a way out of the world. We all went to mass, except Ellie.

Even Michael's free-and-easy style, which brought him adventures with many girls and older women, was only a rebellion against his true nature. If not, why did he come home and drink himself rotten till Pa bashed him senseless, chained him to the bedstead, hand and neck, and left him there to sober up in the cramps of next morning?

Nothing less than love could have led to the climax of Earnshaws' paddock, those strapped, lacerated corpses sprawled for anybody to witness the shame of their ignorance.

In the world of our sty, in among the real pigs which we were, ran the squealing squabbling piglets we gave birth to: butting greedy little appetites, the clatter of jealousies on trotters that might one day be chopped off, stewed, and set cold in gelatine for a polite picnic lunch

at the races, tiny clenched brains and pumping hearts to
be grilled for breakfast or stuffed and baked on festival
days. Even while we bowed our heads at the big table
for Pa to say grace, the floor squirmed with lascivious
snufflings and nips, the brush of a sprung flesh tail against
your bare leg, the odour of insatiability and the wild confusion of an equality in squalor. The respectable silence
of beasts devouring a beast above the board floated thick
as oil on the pandemonium of what was being stifled
below.

Why should we need anyone outside the family? We
had a full-time job playing the games we did. Pigs are
well known as cannibals if they get the chance. The outsiders we did meet seemed pale and too simple. They said
yes if they meant yes, they said please, and when they
expected you to say thank you they also expected that you
intended thanking them. They teased us with tentative
sex, the passes of men wearing boxing gloves, of women
who will blush if their fish-eyes so much as slip to notice
your body. With their mechanisms of work and play, un-
earned loyalty and fatuous opinions, how could they
imagine we would have patience to suffer their childish
advances twice, let alone with enjoyment? While we
waited, marooned on the gaunt rock of such contact, for
a single dry sign of what they intended, the tempest at
home raged without us: Mum loomed from the depths
of the larder, heavy with accusations that would be
exacted in blood; Pa out there, abandoning the horses to
their own company, swung the whip on his own sons for

having fouled up the job of gentling a new stallion; the healing attentions of the girls worked their erotic balm on wounded flesh; and our taciturn speech was offered merely as punctuations in the flood of what could never be spoken because it was too intense, too complex, too intelligent for anyone to talk their way out of if once they got into it.

Such was nature's punishment on Mum and Pa. They knew. They never put this into words, nor did we. But they felt the little piglets butting round them, caught thick complications in the air, they smelled the stench all right. They knew we could never find anywhere interesting after this. They knew we would never let them be free of us.

So, when Artie Earnshaw strode in with his innocence of a young father, his concern at being the bringer of evil tidings, our parents put up the shutters against him, barricaded their privacy, and manned the loopholes with loaded firearms. They knew this was no release. They knew it would not be a question of three burdens, three reminders, the less; but that the murders raised our power over them far enough beyond control for their paradise to go under and never be recovered.

They had hung on to the shreds of innocence, the possibility that one day they might chance back into the magic circle. But now, I'm sure they knew, no innocence could survive. So why should they be in any hurry to set eyes on their disaster? God had aimed this at them.

Sitting round the oil-lamps of a winter's night, Pa read *Lives of the Saints* at the rate of about one sentence an hour. Mum read even more dreadful things in the darkness beyond her own familiar dark. And we played a card game called Happy Families.

When the wind blew from the north-east, which it often did, we could hear a distant crash of waves down at the cliffs below the twenty. And when we had gone to bed—as we preyed on each other, breathing each other's snores, turning together in our separate sleep so our bed-springs made harmony or screamed in someone else's nightmare—the cracks between the planks of the rough walls gaped wider and hair-fine glints of a silver sheet turned its wave to our drowning eyes; our bodyheat went sleepwalking till the dogs grew restless and put up their pointed noses and the horses, musing as they stood round in mockery of sleep, bent to stir the fog with caressing tongues and shook magnificent necks in the moonlight of a mare's eye. While the ocean, that relentless heart, beat beat beat away at the rocks.

Like me, Norah chose a bed next to the wall. And in the morning I would pick splinters from the palms of my hands.

Michael and Willie slept in my room. Michael forever climbing out of the window, thrashing about in the greenery over by the chookyard, sneaking back panting and slicked with dew, forever arcing and humping under his blanket, gasping, grunting, letting slip eels of satisfaction, smelling and damp with his strong body turned to the wall, swinging back to catch me awake, and groaning: Oh Pat if you only knew, if you only knew! and then going off in a spasm that threw him almost out on the floor, while Willie sank silently into the pool of his wondering, diving without a ripple to dredge up some single simple waterlogged version of knowledge—a singlet, a sock—and wake from the very posture he fell asleep in the night before. He'd open his eyes as blank as the morning sky and shake his clubbed brains till he got a basic pattern clear: obedience. He'd put his ugly white feet out and let them scout around like a couple of blindmen for his boots.

Then I knew it was time for me to go and milk the cows.

The Earnshaws' bottom paddock was eight and a half miles from Paradise—eight from our gate to theirs, plus another half down the old rutted track seaward to where that photograph of a faked ambush by blacks and the dread of a real murder of family happened.

We let Artie set off well ahead of us, for the sake of form. When we were ready, our tyrant gathered up the flags and tatters of his victories, clamped his hat tight like a helmet, and mounted to lead us on a retreat into village impertinences. He turned his back on the territory where he, having transformed his father's subsistence scratching, produced meat and honey for the slaves who kept him imprisoned there among his splendours. Mum was already seated passive and ruthless as a church in our new sulky, which I was to drive. Hers was the magnetism that held us; while he dragged the whole lot along in his train, his customary knives and axes lustrous as he urged us on with

the war-weary gesture of impatience, once he had begun,
to see this duty done. Black flames tore at his sleeve. He
whipped up a wind, with his heels dug into the stallion's
startled flanks, an old scent of danger marshalling his
body to heroic massiveness. I was proud of him. And
proud of driving my mother, who sat secret as the Ark of
the Covenant, gold glimmers among her resting fingers,
her hair black with energy and her eyes black from glimpsing the face of the God who had turned away.

So we came, beggarly and majestic as the Middle Ages
in our patched motley, the longbow of our pride strained
tight and ready to let fly at the first fool to oppose our
grandeur with the triviality of public tears. We rode
through the sliprail gate at Earnshaws', golden dust nest-
ling in creases and brushed on our horses' coats, the slowness of our approach storing its own power—Mum, Polly,
and me in the sulky, plus the others on horseback—a
sable king and his giants come among those whose small
lives were set at a sensation by other folks' deaths. Clear
as a curse, our slowness said: this is not your grieving,
leave us to understand the knotted wrists behind their
backs, the hame strap round the neck, the rubric of a
scratched thigh, the clenched fist and the open hand, the
mortuary of foetid secrets which ought never to be shown.
Our slowness said, as we approached in a squadron: these
are twists of an agony we know but ought never to see lie
still and permanent, made obscene in the formaldehyde of
your amazement. As the sulky jolted over turf, the scene
jolted too—those dead bodies jumping closer, flat on their

backs and bouncing our way as the dead horse with his nose set for hell plunged into a frozen scream of gory light. You want to know how I felt? I felt like a burst of trumpets!

Even our Danny put on his constable's uniform for the ceremony.

Mack (who had fetched Sergeant Arrell) was waiting there to help his wife Polly down from my sulky. Also Barney Barnett, who had broken his oath by getting drunk with the sergeant at the Brian Boru the previous night, stepping forward to freeze his hand in Mum's reclusiveness, fumbling for her arm as if she couldn't crush him by her scorn for his presumption, let alone with her weight. The Earnshaws, senior and junior, stood at a respectful disapproval, judged to a nicety. Beyond them the riffraff of Cuttajo sightseers already shuffled with impatience at our delay, having come from six miles closer, besides being winged by a craving for novelty into the bargain, while beyond *them* the shadows of the ancient Koorie people, men who had collapsed in laughter once because a child called out to warn the white man of their ambush, flitted and fragmented while standing still amid the margin of trees they belonged among.

At last I looked across at Ellen's corpse, back to back with Michael, shimmering fly-wings and humming loud as a harmonium from the wounds of Barney's crow-pecking for the scraps of a notoriety as nearly heaven as anything he'd ever find within his reach. Mum pushed him aside with her shadow of air; and this was a sign for us all to dismount. Except Pa, the king, in his remote high tower, who took off his helmet and let the wind ruffle plumes on his natural head. His stallion opened blood-red nostrils and stamped its hooves at the invasion of death. Down below the cliff obscured by trees, seagulls set up a sudden screeching, wild, angry, and mournful.

My mother looked straight at me. You drove me here, her look said. And I was more afraid of this than of the police investigations.

Barney Barnett went among the townsfolk introducing one of the corpses as his fiancée, while Artie Earnshaw stood aside, deep in mysteries. Old Mr Earnshaw, good neighbour and generous heart that he was, approached to offer what support his family could, without intruding. Mum faced him as one colonel to a rival, equal in nobility. Neither bowed, though both accepted the fatal field as an end to such alliance as they had known before: "Thank you, Jack," she said and dug her heels into the sod, driving her cortège forward to the brink of disaster. She looked first at Michael. She had often seen him laid out before —defeated, smashed about the head—confident he would wake to a fresh gallantry of childishness. Then her pondering mind led her to Norah, whom she had loaded with her tasks of a mother, the mother she herself had no wish to be. Back she came. Slowly she stared into Ellen's staring eyes, Ellen who had at last seen evil and, therefore, ceased to be of any use. The dead eyes no longer flinched at what they opened on, and if the living eyes still could not take in the present, they knew the future clearly enough, in my opinion. Johnnie and Kate hid their nausea against each other's neck. But the rest of us looked. Jerry was the one to speak: "Can you shut their eyes?" he asked Father Gwilym, who shook off his centuries-old decorum and flamed with anger. For a moment the priest appeared insane, cheeks stuck with thorns. He picked on me as the one among our barbarians who might be softened to love of the Lord. "Pat," he said, "come with me."

We walked aside, observing our feet press down and crush the grass. We might have been two men in a conspiracy of condolences. Perhaps the others guessed he wished to instruct me in our duty to the dead. But I began to know something I had never suspected of having happened through the years, which added up to just this moment on just this clear midday: "Give me your hand," he asked when we were a safe distance away. We shook hands . . . mine closing on a disc or coin in his palm. "Take it," he explained, "it is yours." And I saw the flames were not anger but shame. I thrust my fists deep in my trouser pockets as we strolled on, just as I often did when I had nothing to hide.

I served at the altar for years without knowing who I served. If I'd asked him at the time, he would undoubtedly have answered in his beautiful foreign voice: Why, boy, the good Lord, our Heavenly Father! And I might have been deceived into accepting this. I loved those winter mornings when the little church floated out of the dark and my pony put on an act of being blown as I let her wander round the verge of the graveyard to browse while

I ran in at the last minute to where Father fretted, already
waving impatiently at me to be ready to help with the alb,
while he took the amice, kissing it and placing it a moment on his head before doubling it back to the collar of
his cassock with practised dexterity, crossed the cords,
right over left, and tied them, giving off an odour of clean-
ness which was not quite the right smell for a man. He
thrust one arm into the alb, then the other, as I danced
round like Norah did when she fitted sister Polly's wedding gown, teasing the cloth so it fell evenly, two finger-
widths from the floor. Next came the moment I knew he
always found fresh. He interrupted the vesting prayers he
had been reciting under his breath—and turned to look at
me in that longing manner of a person given over to the
freedoms of piety: "The cincture, Patrick?" So I'd pass
him the girdle. Sometimes his hands were damp as he
took and tied that symbol of the bonds of Christ fiercely
tight. Finally, he would present himself for my inspection, resplendent in his red chasuble, if this was Pentecost,
with its whiskers of frayed gilt thread.

Then we would be out in the open church, surprisingly
large, timber creaking like a ship at sea, arched ribs above
us, and still the lovely sickening candle fumes and spent
incense. Opening the missal, he escaped my gaze (as I
reconstruct the scene), his voice, magnified, coming back
from the roof as words fit for God: *Introibo ad altare Dei.*
And my own shy piping, because I knew I could never do
justice to his gold and jewelled ritual: *Ad Deum qui
laetificat juventutem meam* . . . while out there in the

scrub kangaroos went crashing through undergrowth and some fellow's dog barked big excited dwindling barks. Then the first two worshippers arrived, wrapped against the cold, and knelt, choosing places widely separate, bowing their heads darkly. All this came back to me when we paced the inquisition of our return to my family, bearing what we knew and could never tell. Father Gwilym and I, linked now not just by the laws of man but in the judgment of heaven.

As we drew close I saw Jeremiah, to my amazement, wiping away tears. So the least likely among us had been able to show grief.

On special days we took a picnic to the beach, which was only a quarter of an hour's walk from our house. We sat there on the sand to eat, when we were small, and ran away to play in the caves, chasing bats out, or we went shooting rabbits along the cliff line. We never took our clothes off. Not one of us could swim. As we grew up we came to think of sand as a nuisance. Till we only went because the ocean was a thing to be seen.

Ellen once jumped from some rocks into a pool. She came up coughing and laughing, her pinafore and petti-coats stuck to her body in a way I could never get out of my mind. She was fifteen then and well shaped, though never to be beautiful like Norah. Michael went mad with fury, he said he should whip her if he had brought Pa's whip. Mum looked on from her recess out of the sun, with never a word. And Pa appeared more interested by Michael's sudden temper than by the dripping, hiccupping girl, who declared it tasted like blood, a big swill of nothing but blood.

Most of us looked at Norah to see how she would take this. We felt she had to be protected because time was slipping through her fingers. Outsiders had begun referring to her as our spinster, a taunt Polly instigated in some flash of spite, because of her own apparent barrenness, no doubt.

On Christmas night (I'm talking about 1898 again now), when Michael hung chained to the bed, dribbling and dozing with his nightmare strung up to dry, Jerry came to sleep where Michael belonged because Mack had taken *his* bed. Jerry had not been in our room for six years. He was twenty, as I've reported previously. So when he did walk in, he filled it. Willie already snored from that corner, and the lamp on my table burned. I had just settled. He said he did not want to come. But now he was there, he stood in full view and stripped. The night, hot as usual at Christmas, crowded in. He wore only a waistcoat and shirt. He flung the waistcoat aside, then tugged the shirt, one of Norah's professional linen shirts, over his head and dropped it out of sight on my floor in the shadow of the table edge. His braces hung down in loops either side, I remember. He kicked off his boots, sending them flying under my bed to thud against the wall and raise a little cry of alarm from Norah awake on the far side. Then he looked at me to be sure I watched, and undid his fly. The thick soft trousers fell in a sudden heap. My younger brother stepped free of them and, at the same time, one

pace nearer me. I should explain quite honestly, that I
was envious. Since he had become a man, I had seen no
more than his arms and his neck. Now he filled our room
with the tranquil forms of giant strength. This was the
Hercules that Father Gwilym showed me in his book of
world art, except Jerry was much younger in the face. The
heat of his calm choked our small privacy to suffocation.
His carved form, heavy as marble, glimmered in lamp-
light. He could overpower me with one hand, and insisted
I should know it. But he didn't even need that one hand:
he didn't need to move. His genitals hung, turning slightly
on an axis, the balls shifting against one another in their
firm bag. Jeremiah, who had never laughed, any more
than Pa, began to smile. By this I knew he knew what I
was thinking. He stood a long time with nothing happening apart from his smile and that slight but terrible
business setting his limp parts shifting ever so gently. I
could not prevent myself thinking it was as thick round
as Norah's wrist. Then I prayed she did not have her eye
to the crack, as I sometimes did from my side. I dared not
stop looking, because his silence forced me to what he
wanted, forced me to study everything, from the huge
shapely feet to a mop of curly hair flopping round his
ears. Maybe half an hour he stood in the hot night, maybe
an hour, while he watched me lose every confidence I had
in myself; he watched the questions of my virgin anticipation and courage rise and subside, my hairy Irish limbs
stiffen and sag. He stood in my room till he was sure he
had driven me back into adolescence by crushing my self-

respect. Then he turned his back on me, the back, if anything, more massively plain, more matchlessly ideal than
the front, and stepped over Michael's bed; he threw off
the sheets as much as to say he would not soil his beautiful
body by contact with them, and lay on the bare mattress,
despite its deeper stains of longing. Lay, face up, aware
he still had me mesmerized, but not looking at me now,
the smile fixed where it had grown. It was the strangest
performance I ever witnessed, and ruthlessly brotherly.
To be such a man, he had left me nothing but my boyhood
and the sweet gravelly escapades of a boy's despair at
making anything add up. That was Jeremiah for you.
Next morning, when I awoke, only his heavy hollows remained in Michael's mattress, and Michael, discarded it
seemed, with that sordid little dump of sheets kicked into
one corner as the victor strode back to his own world.

After I brought the milk pail to the kitchen and set it
down for Norah, who cooked our breakfast, she would
not meet my eyes. I knew then that she had been watching. Jeremiah's smile might not have been directed just at
me. This smile came to mean more than I had feared.

When we swung off home, leaving the murdered bodies behind, we had grown smaller. I no longer felt the jubilation in our strangeness. Success had diminished us. Jeremiah, as the new master, stayed behind to oversee the police enquiries and the bodies being covered. Our Danny joined him, Constable Daniel Murphy, appropriately in uniform and suddenly on duty, though no one asked him in.

Pa as a high stone tower grated on his iron seating, still with the hat in his hand like a weapon, his stallion's haunches shuddering from an encounter with knowledge.

A sudden sheet of fish-scale clouds sliced the sky off high above us, dimming our gold-dust and blurring the fringes of pennants and favours. How ugly we were with our inaccessibility intact, our finery dirty from yesterday's race meeting, the trail of something shabbier than grief being tugged through the air behind us like a net drawn briefly sparkling from the lake only to be seen fouled with weeds and the saturated jetsam of human occasions. I suspect Danny was glad to see the back of us. Mack (yes, even those devoid of moral stature felt their ascendancy at hand) showed how our behaviour shocked and gratified him by sending Polly home the way she had come, with me and Mum, claiming to have some business in town before he could join us. "Business at the Brian Boru, I dare say," I muttered as he baggaged his wife in a frill of silly snivels.

I looked back once, to see flies spread their pearly veil above the sergeant's head while he resumed cross-examining the corpses. What could be done? Wind drummed about us. "A murdered body is the possession of the Crown," Sergeant Arrell had said, "so it is my duty to take the deceased in charge." More drums. He squinted up at the chinks in Pa's craggy face. No response. "I shall have them taken," he announced further, "to the pub and locked up safely."

It was while we were riding away amid dust gone rusty that our neighbour Artie (so I was to hear later from Daniel) brought the sergeant a valuable exhibit, a hefty lump of hardwood, four feet long and four inches thick. On the end of this weapon he displayed splats of blood and a trace of brains. Together the men fitted this club to each crushed skull and found it perfect. Arrell observed that an ordinary man could wield the weapon only by using both hands, and tried it through the air. Jeremiah offered to disprove this theory. Apparently he took hold of it with one hand, and gave a mighty swipe, which just missed the sergeant's own head. The crowd, it seems, moved closer for a better look at what had done the damage. But I only have this on hearsay. What I remember was our hunched forms of plague-victims, the wind at our backs showing our clothes as the tatters of a discredited rabble, and Jeremiah riding up behind, manoeuvring his horse alongside the sulky, his face wearing an appearance of anguish or perhaps illicit satisfaction. Then he presented me with a contemptuous smile, his smile of the night before. I have never felt so helpless to be myself. This was worse than anything. He smiled as a man smiles at a child with whom he shares a secret so damning it cannot be spoken without the man demeaning his manhood or the child surrendering the immunity from punishment afforded him by ignorance.

Once back at home, we installed Mum indoors, where she belonged. The horses whinnied the stench of death out of their nostrils. The creek slid past, as it had for aeons before our place was built; she-oaks growing in white sand on the banks whispered murder. This was where I took my horses, in among agitated accusations, to let them drink their fill, to watch them raise dripping velvet muzzles and shake their manes now and again, before returning them to the home paddock ready for saddling later in the afternoon.

By the time I stamped up the two steps and passed through those invisible walls of our public privacy, Mum had dressed herself in a terrific grief of betrayal. Lightnings flashed from her moodiness. Her hands clubbed at her own unyielding flesh, which was too thickly packed to show any sign of distress. Tears spurted from her eyes in surprised bursts. Did she, for the first time, truly see herself as alone? How shall I describe such forlornness? Previously she had moved in the gloomy halo of a person shut out from herself and patiently knocking at a private door to be admitted again, avoiding distractions by keeping her back to the world. But now, you could see straightaway, when she had turned round and no longer knocked, the secret door swung open and some inner woman dragged her outer self right in, shooting the bolts behind her; so she had appeared at a window to weep and rage against injustice. She had, at the same time, become more shut away and yet able more openly to see us. Clearly we came in range of her fury. She began shouting between the sobs, and thunders of an autocrat despite her husband: "I suppose I shall have to do all the mending myself!"

I had arrived in time to watch her turn her frenzy against poor Polly: "How did that butcher of yours know where to find them?" she demanded with all that this might mean, and sent Polly staggering from the house, screaming down to the creek till the horses cantered in wild circles round the rails, their great eyes rolling, soft mouths hardening to blackened brass fanfares.

Pa contributed only one thing, but not about the butcher: "He thinks he has taken over."

So I had not been the only one to see what I saw in Jeremiah.

Mum, finding she was no longer just part of Pa, shot him this discovered look of hers.

"Wasn't it enough," she asked, "for Michael to be chained all night to our bed and myself kept from sleeping by his moans?"

Reliving it, she added something more.

"And the feel of his flesh going heavy?"

Then we knew the home at Paradise had broken for good and all. Pa, fossilized in his chair at the head of the table, never moved. He sits there to this day, anchoring our house, preventing it from being blown away in a southerly gale.

Sergeant Arrell fired a question at me the moment I put my head in the door of the Brian Boru later that afternoon: "And when did you last see your sisters and your brother alive?"

The bar had been screened off into a partly private cubicle. Sunlight bounced off the bay outside. These tall stained screens shed a dull mirrored light into the true mirrors of a great sideboard behind the bar. Here the world fitted into neat recesses backed with smaller square mirrors, in each of which passers-by outside the window flickered through the distorting bubble of a near-empty spirits bottle. The sea's repetitions slid down bevelled glass edges through filaments of red-orange, green-indigo. Great beer taps jutted above the bar, forsaken for the present. Disgruntled regulars were directed round the back to the illegal door they normally used only after closing time. A voice was heard to repeat at intervals:

"There's bodies in here, mate. Yeah, bodies. Round the back you'll be able to get a drink. Well, there's been murders."

Sergeant Arrell sat on the kitchen chair they must have brought him specially for his rank. He waited. I answered.

"I met them on the road."

He said (and I watched the back of his head in the mirror beyond): "After they had been to the dance?"

"Before."

He said (the back of his head appearing to belong to a different man altogether and one not at all clever): "Were you travelling in the same direction or going the other way?"

"After the races they went home. But I didn't. I had promised Sister Veronica to shift her holiday garbage. And I'd promised to check the lamps for her before too late. So I rode straight on to Cuttajo, instead of stopping at home on the way. I was at the convent by five-and-twenty past seven. It took me about an hour to put things right for the Sisters. I did look in at the hall to check how they were going with the dance, but the girls told me only three people had turned up so far. All men."

The sergeant nodded (and the mirror grew lighter, then darker, then lighter, with the coloured edges of a white sea framing him). He didn't need to ask who I meant by the girls. He had been in our community a long time. He knew that Father Gwilym's little band of fiddlers played for our amusements as well as in church.

"I decided not to stay, even if the others did, so I rode back home. About two miles down the track I met them coming the other way. They were singing, and this meant Michael was half-drunk on something, though where he got it I couldn't say. His rum was taken off him the night before, you see. We stopped and had a yarn. And I went on my way. Except for my horse going lame, I would have been home in another half hour."

Sergeant Arrell thought a moment, perhaps about the lame horse, then pursued his line of questioning: "I understand they arrived at the hall at ten minutes past nine to find it shut and the dance cancelled?"

"That I don't know."

A door opened behind me (in the mirror it looked like a door opening in his head).

He told me in the voice of a judge: "I shall want to question you further, Patrick."

In came the doctor, who had travelled all the way from Bunda as soon as he got news on the telegraph. Dr Heinrich von Lossberg, his name was, government medical officer, plus a high speaker for German science and modern knowledge of all kinds. His shadow hopped from one mirror to another as he went straight to the corpses. Then I turned to watch him, aware that it would look unnatural not to be able to face what he was doing. He lifted the raincoat put to cover their battered heads. He dropped it straight back again.

"Sergeant Arrell," he reported in a military manner,

yet with soft corners of melancholy, "I came as fast as possible."

Arrell handed him an empty .38 cartridge. The doctor took it and turned slightly away from me to examine what he had taken. The big mirror showed his heavy, pale, concerned but unmoved expression. His mouth shaped itself for the beginnings of some intelligence, but he held back. Then he glanced up. And we were, without warning, eye to eye in the glass.

Once, during my special lessons, Father Gwilym had guided my hand with his cold fingers, to read for myself (he treated me as a blind person) the answer to my question. I had put it to him that butchers speak of themselves as set above other trades and I could see no justification for this. He consulted his shelves of books, more crowded than the School of Arts Library, going filmy like a bad eye and reading the spines with his fingers. Once he made his decision, the place grew calm as a monastery. He announced that I would have to search back to times before Christ to find an answer to what I wished to know.

In the first book he laid open on my lap was a lithograph of a pagan priest holding a long knife over a lamb tied to an altar. Then, some pages later, another sacrifice—this time, if I remember aright, in the Americas, where the victim was human. His finger wiped a few

specks of dust from the page so I could see more clearly
the healthy man chained to a grid, much as Michael had
been chained in sight of us all on his rowdy occasions.
This priest brandished a cleaver.

Father Gwilym's voice came feverish as his hand was
cold: "In pagan times, priest and butcher were one and
the same man."

He stole the book back, though I had not seen enough,
and put another in its place. This was a bulky volume of
annotations concerning the Jewish faith. He explained,
voice boiling and bubbling from the excitement of knowing such matters: "Even to this day the kosher butcher is
charged with draining the blood from all meat because
an Orthodox Jew must not take blood into his body and
has to be confident the butcher is trained in the rituals and
understands the articles of faith, so his meat will be properly prepared and fit to eat. Here you will find," he flipped
some pages, "a list of the religious knowledge a kosher
butcher must learn," he snapped the volume shut in a
sudden hurry. "Our modern butchers," he smiled re-
motely, "remember to claim special respect for their
trade but forget what they ought to know to earn it."

The thought of Mack sitting through a course of theological studies made me laugh out loud.

He asked: "Do you recall how you used to intone the
responses to the litany for me? You were shy. No one
else gave them out half so beautifully. Whenever I came
to *Dominus vobiscum* you always hesitated. Did you
worry that you wouldn't get it right? Whatever the

reason," his cold fingers flew onto mine and perched there, "your *Et cum spiritu tuo,* addressed to me as priest of course, sounded specially for me as a person. As if you hoped . . ."

He sighed and his eyes grew old. I noticed the worn cuffs of his cassock. I am cursed with sentimentality. His voice faded, so faint and so suggestive you could believe it was compounded of imperfect echoes whispering back original words which still remained, somehow, unspoken.

He confessed regretfully: "My own sin was vanity."

There were still other things I needed to know about the butcher.

Wherever you looked, McNeil had been there first; he was the one to offer his horse and sulky for the expedition to the dance, he was the one who volunteered to search for the missing revellers next morning, and he found them in that out-of-the-way spot without a moment wasted on indecision.

Was it that the butcher saw the dignity of the tragedy? Did he, because of his trade, recognize that these were no longer family bodies but sacrificial offerings to some public hunger? Whatever the reason, he did not ride back to Paradise to allow the kin of those who'd died to be the first with the grief of it—he went straightaway to seek out the figures of authority, policeman and priest. And when the squadron of our dark closeness drifted away on a clutter of horse hooves, stirred as trees are stirred, who was it brushed an eager Barney Barnett aside and undertook to cart the cadavers to Cuttajo and lay them out but

this man whose every working day refined his expertise
in handling dead flesh, hefting the hollow carcases he
would dismember with ceremonial precision, fastidious
(yes, I allow him this at least) as a priest dabbing fingertips on a cloth after having anointed the orifices of living
senses.

What were those two women to him, even without
his leather cap of office? Why just the women? He left
the male corpse to others, so I gathered in the illegal bar
at the Brian Boru that afternoon. And wasn't it the
butcher who stopped his mouth when I entered, though
he did not yet know I had been asked to leave the front
bar while Dr von Lossberg flew in on his travelling
cape, togged up for an Alpine crossing though our holiday weather was stifling as usual. Milky heat from the
Pacific broke white and tumultuous around the little hotel, swirling dirt aloft and lashing windows with a storm
of dead bird-cries. High above my back, that flat skin of
fish-scale cloud spread from horizon to horizon. These
minutes were the inner pulsing and fury of a great creature swimming across the sky, digesting us as it went, our
agony a mere symptom of well-being for that irresistible
headlong rush away from all we had known.

The butcher's hands, upraised, spoke for him the words
he now held back. I hardly recognized my brother-in-law
filled thus with the power of office, his face moulded to a
celebrant's fierce impartiality. I had seen this look before,
when Father Gwilym escaped the small bother of following me with his eyes as I corrected his alb and he emerged

into the church, past the bleeding heart of Jesus, glancing once, always, at the Virgin and then loosing his voice to soar on the mystery of *Introibo ad altare Dei* . . . even the mild Father and his bloodless hands mighty with that cry, becoming part of a universal invocation uttered without cease all round God's earth, his voice simply joining what was already there, the thin tone natural to him swelling to ring vigorously with some power he called from our imprisoned longings. So the silence and upraised arms, shocking as the blow of a great bell, deafened us.

"I'd ask you," the butcher spoke again at last, "to observe a minute's silence in respect for the dead ones under this roof."

I stood there at the back doorway, restrained by ritual, while he escaped from what he might have been saying. Now it has been explained to me I see it all. Now I have been reminded of my lesson so many years before in the heritage of butchery, the time I laughed. Here, with my sisters and brother murdered, that immemorial tradition revived.

In spring, when bats wheeled round the house at night whistling, and in the morning dry gum leaves fell from the trees as dead wings, Willie came running down to where I worked repairing the fence in the south-east corner of the twenty. I scarcely knew him for the singing birds in his lightness.

He always kept weasels. He bred them in cages at one side of the stables. We took them rabbiting. Ever since I was a boy he had had them. After his beating and the loss of his wits he clung to their dependence on him; weasels were the ones he talked to in his mumble of a big dry tongue and broken teeth. They fought and clamoured for him just as if nothing had happened, and whatever else his brain no longer knew, he knew the sense of this— he was still their master and provider, still the one to risk his bare hands among those needle teeth, the one to choose which should mate with which in the piss-damp straw. He was the one to watch them do it in their miniature Eden and be satisfied by the squirm of litters. He knew how it was done. He knew the responsibility of guiding their lives to his purpose. He had that lordly impassiveness of deciding this *meant* nothing.

Mum, who drew the family about her sombre magnetism to have us at mass with her, took to leaving Willie at home since she noticed him unexpectedly living his private life during the service, deaf to the littleness of anything unnecessary to his inner order of holding chaos in check. He grunted during the preparation of the host, he appeared not to notice how beautifully her favourite served at the altar (Pat), he spoke simple horse noises through the Benedictus and jumped the claim of the Dies Irae by pushing his way free of suffocation among men and women, stumbling, falling, scrambling up and charging towards the open portal and out to liberty with a bellow of suppressed pain. The lopsided wreckage of his damaged brain lived it all, the inward hypnotism as a fixed focus behind his wandering eye. But this spring morning on the crackling leaves of that little copse in the gully where I was cranking some new wire tight, he called out to me in a voice resurrected from earlier times: "Patrick, Patrick!" and his bright tragedy fixed on me so powerfully I felt I must wrestle against his shadow, that his bottled-up strength would make even Jeremiah tremble for the family's fate. His young voice called me to account: "Patrick, come home straightaway, Mum's dead!"

I suppose I must have looked up in unmasked amazement, because he recollected himself and his fate of never knowing. The dull toad settled in his cheeks, his excited hands grew to lumps and weighed him off balance till that limber running of youth-regained tripped him and he crashed sidelong against the harp of my morning's work. Lurching off the wire, he blurted a horse-grunt in my face, hot nostrils spread wide and yellow with fear. But I was not fooled. The wild fellow who had once needed beating senseless to slow him down had escaped control in those moments, had shown himself and could not be taken back. A lifted blind revealed the Willie I remembered, proud as a man should be, the one we took our troubles to when we didn't go to Norah. I'd almost forgotten, because I was only nine when Pa crushed his ribs for daring to say he would walk away and live his own life . . . and then being woken in bed to see my lamp flare at the passage of rushing bodies, Willie gripping a knife and the flash of blood across Pa's shoulder, as he was in the act of delivering that terrible blow to silence us all and shut our heads in the muffling of Willie's idiocy, so even when we walked straight we knew it was by the grace of Pa that we didn't totter like our elder brother. I had forgotten in the intervening years, but this reminded me.

For the first time since the murders, I wondered what Willie was capable of, what might be woken in him at any moment, pent with the superhuman energy of all he had to stifle to live as our household idiot, what fury of cunning might thrust up under the lid of the simple tasks he confined himself to.

Only now do I begin to understand my father's anger. He had arranged a world for us where we could be free of the usual creeping lassitude, free of rudderless bewilderment on a sea of possibilities, free from the corruption of choice—a world in which each of us had a secure place. Australia was going soft, he saw that, and he kept us hard. We raised our own beef, we made cheese and stored it, bred chickens, and grew the fruit and vegetables we ate. Even Willie the simpleton knew the feel of this vision, had taken it in his hands once, used it as a weapon, and failed. Pa let Polly escape the boundaries of his contempt because she could never be brought to understand. She thought Paradise was just a little farm where she happened to have been born, and grew to hang round on the verandah mooning for some oaf to carry her off to parties so she might tittle-tattle and envy other females' frills. Polly was a waste of time. That's why he let her go and even came good with a sulky to seal the bargain.

On the other hand, what if, instead, Pa had wanted to lure the butcher in? What if Polly's vamping was exactly what his kingdom required, sunlight catching the skin of her caged young body and momentarily dazzling her lover. Had any words been said when the butcher arrived in his Sunday suit, with a collar tight round his neck as a hame strap, new braces sandpapering against the starch of his shirt, all studs and strained seams, his square head heavy with the arcane calligraphy of veins his knife must follow, about how to split skulls in a manner pleasing to God?

As for William, the fact is that each child is born into a different situation even if all are born in the same household. The youngest are inheritors of rights won by those who came before. The eldest has the task of teaching his parents. Through his rebellions and illnesses, and more than anything else through his trust, he takes the raw dominance of father and mother (not even yet accustomed to the single skin they have come to inhabit as a pair) and defines their greatness for them, taking upon himself the punishment this entails. They rage against captivity and he must accept the blame, they turn violent with inadequacy and he is the scapegoat, because he is the master. Any wonder then that after twenty years of following where Willie led and facing all the trials he posed, Pa finally took rebellion into his own hands and set the question of mastery where he intended it should remain. We all learnt a lesson we never forgot. Without needing to think this out, we made Willie our special care. We looked after him and saw to his comfort in small ways. From that day on, he never lacked the harvest of his brief doomed period as the Pretender. Michael's turn came next; then Norah's, in a different way; then Daniel's, though something about Daniel warned our parents he was a cuckoo's child and not to be trusted or mistaken for one of their own, because right from the start he wore Pa's name all wrong; then mine.

But, of course, Michael still held out. Thanks to Michael, none of the rest of us had to take the full brunt. There began to be support for the task of civilizing Mum and Pa. Also, something else intervened before the succession could come down to me. Jeremiah outgrew me. But I am wandering from the point. The question now became: Could Willie have wanted to strike back at those who gained from his young lifetime of striving and loss?

Pa made for us an infamy, without which we would have been in rags. We were the tribe of the savage Paradise. Boys at school had feared us long before they met us. What other family in the district was spoken of in an undertone? The priest's housekeeper warned him no good would come of having me as altar boy; I overheard her and then walked into that room boldly. Where had I learned to be bold? I knew it in my blood. Afraid and ashamed as I was, by the very fact no good was to come of me, I had to live up to my name. A light grew in

Father Gwilym's eye. As of that moment, he fancied me;
whereas he had merely been willing to give me a try
before, because the other fellows proved unreliable. He
had his own pride of office, and at that instant we were
in league against the housekeeper and her respectability.
But, more remarkable, we were equals in this compact.
My family's reputation obliged me to perform the rites as
perfectly as could be—then I was sure to keep the gossips
guessing, then they would watch me closely, following
every least action, not to miss the moment of my breaking
out. They never grew weary of this. Isn't that remarkable?
In their conformity they could not change their minds.
And if any were tempted to do so out of charity,
Mum's weekly appearance at mass put a stop to that.
Black hair tied in a strict bun and her strict black eyes
black with what she saw of the respectable society which
shunned her, she moved a tabernacle of funereal pride
wherever she went, and blossomed nobly with a spirit so
challenged.

You have nothing, her look spoke clearer than words,
but trinkets!

The entire town speculated on what she might say in
the confessional. So did we children. Pa, if he ever went,
would have a good deal to own up to, including rages,
whippings, and triumphs, glorying in the power he had
taken, blasphemy, and boundless pride. But our mother,
what did she ever do that she could put a name to and
ask penance? Was the thickness of the air around her an
offence? Was her rank seething fertility to be laid to her

own charge? Had she invented the simple words of the English language she used? Mum clouted us, including the girls from time to time, but never in the fury of recognition; she did it absently, a reflex of the arm to some meaningless stimulus, because she would not allow us to interrupt her, she would not even be distracted into interrupting herself. Her whole concentration was on something neither good nor evil and therefore no matter for confession. How many Hail Marys, how many No-venas would need to be paid for having ceased to observe that evil was an option? What penance could she do for forgetting she had ever had a life before she married Pa? Her uprightness being in no way doctrinaire, it was with-out moral value. Mum remained as she was because she had no imagination. Even when she barged past the butcher's helping hand as she trod heavily down from the trap, the vehicle dipping to that side and springing back level once she was safely adrift on the soil, I think she hadn't the imagination to believe her daughters and her son were dead. She could see the corpses, yes, the wounds, a blanket spread under Michael and Ellen with patches of their blood soaked into it and ants feeding: but she saw it as the ants saw it, she could not imagine it into any reality of being obscene.

She would not have them come to her again, nor hear their voices, of course she knew this. But now life had left them, she couldn't work her reflexes round to the fact that they were ever anything different. Events had simply caught up with some intuition she might have felt, so Mum recognized the corpses with a frankness she could not spare them while they were alive and making demands on her to know what she could not ever know without pushing past the frontier of things one can grasp in one's hand. Her limit of pain was this. Also her limit of contentment. She could not catch hold of sympathy, so she had none. Ought she to have been punished for it? Mum had had uses for those three; she needed to think how to reorganize the house duties as soon as she could get home. Her role in Pa's kingdom was as its unquestioning heart. Four months later, she astonished us at supper. Suddenly she said: "When the first of them was killed the other two must have watched, so one poor soul watched it twice." Her darkness quivered and a bright film fled across her eyes.

She was dead, herself, next morning.

The disgraceful scene in the illegal bar at the Brian Boru Hotel erupted out of the bare branches of a dream plumtree suddenly flowering such multitudes of white anger the dangerous bees worked crazily to stuff their trouser pockets full of pollen before it all flew away in a final explosion of deathly perfume. If the tree had still been alive, it ought to have carried loads of fruit at that time of year. But stuck beside the back fence, where everyone pissed and threw up their surfeit of alcoholic poisoning, it had died. I was gazing at it when suddenly I found myself looking *through* it, between branches where the blossoms popped into focus as men's eyes gleaming with resentments which went deeper than the inconvenience of being shut out of the front bar. The sea's milky heat flecked their hungers. The butcher, with arms upraised to still a storm of grit lashing windows and walls, called for a minute's silence to save his own skin, because he knew I knew he had been talking about our family disrespectfully.

The eyes were not on him. The eyes were, every one, on me. And this was how I knew. Eyes which had nothing to hide or fear, all together as they were in that swarm, weighed down by the honey of belonging. This promised to be a real Donnybrook.

I took my glass of ale when the minute was up and would have drunk it quietly while their suspicions raged round them and stung them with the lust to know. Simply as brother of the victims, I enjoyed a stature their quelled passions envied. They would have stuck needles into me and sucked my blood if that might slake their thirst for what they knew they would never know. But from a secret corner of the squalid room, Artie Earnshaw's cousin spoke up: "You shouldn't have left it all to us," he said . . . meaning, as every man understood, the carting of the bodies into town.

"Is that you, Barney?" I replied, squinting at the muck of what little light pushed that far in. "I thought you had intentions of carrying my sister off, in any case!" I said this because all the way back home in our cavalcade one thing jolted and jostled before my mind's eye—the sight of Barney Barnett rushing to be first to get at Ellen's corpse, putting his arms round her stiff resistant body to heave her away from Michael, making an awkward job of it, his boots scuffing the dirt and his face cooked in a fire of lewdness. He had not waited for permission. Being her fiancé, he took it as his right, though Artie and the butcher, in the end, did the work.

Barney jumped at me and I put him on his back with a single punch. I knew I had to leave and not return because those words, which had slipped out before I could imagine how they might sound, were not just in heathen bad taste but victorious.

I stood over him, Murphy that I was and a fully paid-up member of the Old King's black vanguard, to make certain he could not accuse me of running away. He knew he was beaten. I'm only surprised he ever tried it on me. "You've been left with nothing, mate," I told him. Again, once spoken, the words sounded wrong. I found I had already set my glass down. So I left it, half-full, where it was. "And you can finish my beer if you like," I added as I went out, hating him because I hated them all.

I tell you one thing: whatever I may have expected to see in my life, never once did this include Barney Barnett as a lonely ruin in his bed, hooking a finger through a hole in his grandma's sheet to keep a grip on life while he skited to the police about how he had been the murderer, urgent in his plea of guilty, anxious to have the purple stole of some grand office authenticate his importance and guide him to eternal life in the annals of infamy.

The Barnetts' farm was the only working property between our place and Earnshaws'. The house stood closer to the paddock where the murders happened than the Earnshaws' own house did. But it was still a good way out of sight. During the enquiry, Barney was asked how he came to be first on the scene after the butcher William McNeil.

"I took that way because my dogs would give me no peace."

"And the dogs led you across the field to your own boundary fence, did they?" the magistrate asked and, when this had been answered in the affirmative, observed that they were singular dogs to scent dead bodies half a mile away when they could not, apparently, hear the screams and shots the previous night at the same distance.

This had Barney sweating to get off the hook, just the way we saw him sweat to get back on it before he pegged out altogether.

Pa nor Mum could bring themselves to answer much more than yes or no to the questions aimed at them, such was their scorn for the shallow life out there in society, including its law courts. The enquiry itself proved they were right to keep us separate from the ruck; even if this had had to be achieved through violence.

Of great interest to the case were some reported scratches on Pa's arms. He was required to lay them bare in evidence, though the marks had entirely healed in the interim. He did so with the dignity of a man who has no option but show his power, though vanity would never seduce him into doing so. The scratches, he explained when pressed, happened on Christmas Eve while clearing a new paddock down along the creek at the far south corner of our place.

It was impossible to imagine how we might have felt if we believed Pa would be put on trial: perhaps excited by something close to recognition. But I don't think so. As I recall, the moment we set foot off Paradise in a bunch, we felt we had risen to our inheritance, the exclusive, marauding clannishness of us. They never bothered interrogating him or me or my brothers on the work we did together, so they missed the whole essence of the family. Without work we were a simple tyranny and fit for pity.

The great project of clearing a new paddock had begun months before. We'd hoped to finish by the beginning of December, but one thing or another delayed the last few acres. "Christmas!" Danny jeered before he left for work in Bunda, "it'll be Christmas before you lot get through that patch of scrub." He was correct, though it cost him a swipe from Pa for saying so and he had to have Norah clean up his uniform again. "Christmas!" said Michael, always cheerful, "we'll swear to have it done by Christmas."

So on Christmas Eve we were down to the very last patch and hell-bent on seeing it through. We got up long before dawn, lamps lit, our shadows clubbing each other in the opposed indignities of sticking arms into unwashed shirts and thrusting our hands out for mugs of steaming tea from Mum's cavernous duty. The beds, behind us now, eased themselves free of our shapes, blankets disordered and thrown back, pillows grey as cold muttongrease. Drifting woodsmoke mingled with an intrusion of the humid outdoors to burrow in our boots waiting on the step for when we had filled our bellies with porridge and tea and shuffled from the kitchen, barefoot and already hot, to tie on our work for the day. Right by Mum's hand, the open firebox of her black stove licked its scavenger's chops, the red raw ribbing inside huffing mouth-warm against her skirt and casting a glow on the cupboard door across the room where dark fugitive legs flickered past. Standing round the cook pot like soldiers on guard duty and feeding without bothering to sit, we ate in our sleep. Far off, the ocean roared in towards land, bringing dawn on its back. A lone wakeful dingo, somewhere down beyond the blacks' camp, crowed tragically once; and minutes later, once again.

Then the day marched in to get us, suddenly brisk and ceremonial. Light chimed against the windows and tramped across the verandah, and threw a gold bar in on the kitchen floor. The fire grew pale. Mum's great shadow shrank, heavy and tricky as mercury. "It's five o'clock," Willie said in the voice of a clock. And Ellen, who was to do my milking chore while I went with the others, picked up two buckets. First down the steps, she was struck by a halo, a flood of sun-rays at eye-level. Lifting one bucket, she shielded her dazzlement with a forearm. Michael galloped in pursuit, scooping his boots off the step on the way and feathering his ankles with a rainbow of assaulted dew. He went a few paces past her and swung round, walking backwards so he could face her while he said whatever it was those flustered pale moths carried up with them into the trees. Then he laughed, probably because he knew Pa would be staring across at him, censorious as a judge, and that Mum must by now have slammed the iron door shut on her dancing fire and dragged the kettle into place with water for scalding the pig still snoring in its pen beyond the scullery door. And I remembered I had to be back home by noon to lend Mack a hand, because he had promised to do the job professionally when he brought Polly to join the girls in decorating our house, in laying out clean linen for the festival, and baking pastries plus an extra batch of bread.

We armed ourselves with axes and saws, and slung the winch in an old trap Pa used my school pony to pull (this was the pony's only job now, in old age). Michael led the big horses up from the creek to meet us at the ford, the shaggy hairs stuck to their fetlocks with clean water. We turned to watch him: Pa and Willie on the job, Jeremiah, young John (then sixteen), and me.

We worked together like a single machine, felling trees, lopping branches, using the stripped trunks to roll the scrub aside, shoulders swelling at the weight, soil on our hands, breaking holes in the sky and filling them with the smoke of demolition. Whipbirds darted about ahead of this progress, clinging low down on unfallen trees, snicking us with the late-coiling thongs of their cry.

It was just such bush that Pa's father first broke into, a forest so thick you worked in it by intuition, hearing a multitude of sounds but seeing little, frogs calling from high among the leaves and the ground alive with animals, furred and scaley tails disappearing beneath the mould just in front of your boots, each axe blow echoing (I thought of a match struck in a maze of mirrors). And beginning with a single tree, his first victim, picked at random, he broke a space for the sun to reach, a space where he and his wife could dig with wooden spades, plant their handfuls of wheat, and then go home in a buoyancy of exhaustion, with the idea of naming the humpy they had built of stacked bark Paradise.

Relentless as a cancer, our grandparents ate into the surrounding scrub, the sunny patch growing large enough for a whole field of wheat. In forty years of slavery, hair falling thick over their shoulders, eyes sparkling alive and ambitious, they cleared a hundred and eighty acres, adding pasture for sheep to their crops; then Pa took over with his grand plan of beef. He bought a block of timbered country to the north, which everybody said was good for nothing, till the pit-sawyers arrived and cut us planks to enlarge the house by a verandah. The gap they felled led straight to the fence between us and the Barnetts. Pa had his eye on a creek out that way, Burnt Bridge Creek, as it was called to commemorate some forgotten mishap maybe higher upstream. The water was good, though not so plentiful as our Blacks Creek, but he chiefly wanted the land for the way it lay. Pa could look at a dense heap of scrub where you'd barely make out what was fifty yards ahead and see it as a place for, say, potatoes.

So, while Barnetts lost hold of their pride and failed by a small margin each year, we Murphys were ready to make an offer on that potato patch along the precious creek. Once we got it, we went in to clear it, singing and slashing, steel blades and winches at work, Pa in the middle, still respectable in his sweat-soaked shirt and waistcoat, heaving trees aside with a silent surly ferocity, now and again checking on his sons as we routed the wildlife to smash forward yard by yard, attacking virgin undergrowth and leaving behind a widening band of mangled leaves, split branches, and raw black soil.

By Christmas Eve the fires had almost died away in huge stumps and hollow charcoal shells of fallen trunks. We were down to raking and piling smaller rubble when Oliver Barnett and his son Barney called over to see what we had done that they had not been able to do. They smoked a pipe with Daniel Junior (the only one among us to have the habit), while he explained that he was home on a couple of days' furlough, just for the festivities.

"Nice job you've made of this, Dan," old man Barnett said to Pa, and I thought how handsomely he rose to the occasion, seeing what he had lost.

"We'll fence her in the new year," Pa agreed, and this

was a lot of talking from him. But he spoke it like he once said to the beaten Willie: Shall I break your leg as well, or leave that till some other time?

Ruin was slow coming to the Barnetts, but it didn't let up. Their folks had arrived with plenty of cash, which they then nibbled their way through, mean as they were and bare of comforts, till it came down to Barney lying on the family bed with his granny's sheet up round his neck, adam's apple a shrivelled fruit long past the time for picking, and his mouth falling open over to one side, showing the white slug inside which the priest would have to dab with chrism while a cracked bell went ringing the alarm: I'm not talking about no bloody horse, I'm talking about him and his sisters!

We didn't invite them over.

Then I said: "Time for me to go. Mack'll be up home." I waited for Pa's permission, and once he had given it some thought he nodded. I dropped my tools in the trap for Willie to drive home that night and set off up the hill. I heard Barney yell: "Hang on." But I never thought he meant me. Next thing, he's panting alongside. "Is it the pig?" he asked. "It's the pig," I replied. He said: "I never killed a pig." I said: "Mack's the butcher." He said: "Can I lend a hand?"

The whipbirds, having nowhere better to go, now we had cleared their corner of bush, whistled frantic whippings around us. He came.

"Dad won't care," he explained, and this was what seemed the most astonishing thing to me.

"We're only having a turkey," he whinged as we reached the road and jogged along, not to be late.

"Are you coming to the races?" he asked, sounding blown.

"I won fifteen bob last year," he laughed boastfully, weakening.

"Ellen promised we'll go in together with the profits," he almost sobbed.

"Listen," Barney Barnett begged as we approached the rise where that stony gully cuts across the road, the very spot Michael drove the sulky at too fast the time he busted the wheel which Mack fixed once it was given to him for taking Polly's gossip out of hearing.

"Shall we walk awhile?" he gasped.

I prided myself on being like iron. I could run home and back to Cuttajo without taking a break, even after a morning's labour. I liked the way I felt. I had him beaten. No one asked for his company. I kept on running while he dropped behind. I didn't once look back. No need. He had been ground into the dust, and I enjoyed the thought of that. I ran on in my work boots, shirt-tail hanging out of my pants and my collar stud missing so the wind ran big warm hands over my chest. I was sweating and I wished somebody would drive along to see me, some wagonette carrying a crowd of females to see my plastered hair and disreputable loose shirt, watch me steam past in a whiff of male smell and later think of me again when they came upon poor broken-winded Barney, hopelessly outclassed back there, probably bent forward, one hand on each thigh like an auxiliary piston, driving his legs straight to help heave himself up the slope. I beat him by a quarter of an hour.

When he arrived through the gate, doing his best to make light of his defeat and glancing round to find out from the ladies' expressions whether I had mentioned him at all, Mack and I were just dragging the pig to where we had set up a frame to bleed him on. Barney's flat voice (whining: "Goodday, Mrs Murphy; goodday, ladies, Mack . . .") brought on the afternoon and hunger. Though I'd promised myself a bite of bread, I had not stopped to have it, and couldn't now. Mack said: "Are you helping too?"

"Too right I am, if I'm let," Barney offered.

"You can do it all by yourself if you're so keen," Mack told him.

"That's our one pig for Christmas," Mum warned from the scullery door. "Don't you boys go spoiling him."

I had worked with Mack before, and we made a quick job of lugging the beast out and lashing it down with the ropes put ready. It had been done this way for centuries in Ireland, using the Kilkenny frame.

Hunger suddenly seized hold of me; my gut raging with emptiness, I saw scarlet lights I mistook for a glimpse of something our ancestors on the far side of the world had handed down to us. Warlike monks in monasteries holding off the Viking marauders, Saint Brigid—buried at Downpatrick beside her dear friend Saint Patrick, and Saint Columba on the other side—Mary the Gael, as

Father Gwilym called her, his voice clouding as it did when he was teaching Edith Earnshaw the violoncello. Mack walked round the victim, inspecting it, his pouch of knives, worn like a sporran slipped sideways onto his hip, clattering, and the steel swung by a cord. He selected one long, pointed blade. The pig watched him hone it, then watched him thinking as he stropped, then screamed at the top of its lungs.

Norah, I knew, hid her head indoors. She could never bear the slaughter. Mum rumbled back to the stove to be sure her great iron kettle kept on the boil. Young Kate in the peartree peeped through a Venetian lattice of fingers, trying to laugh. But of all the women, it was Ellen who caught my attention. From the scullery door she looked at this pig, absorbed in watching it. Even though Barney put on a tough act to make her notice him, she had eyes only for the pig.

"I'll do it this year if you like," I offered, and the hunger in me was a kind of speed, a kind of concentration.

Far away a wakeful dingo answered the howling pig with a howl of its own: the one a desperate betrayed outrage, the other a timeless longing. Ellen's expression changed at that instant from curiosity to what I can only call recognition.

Why he did so, I don't know. But Mack, who was in charge of the job, ignored my claim and handed the knife to Barney, whose pleading, irritable anxiety of a beaten person fell away from him to reveal a champion.

He brandished the knife admiringly, though Ellen still refused to notice. Eager to snatch glory from a life of defeats, he drew his arm back to drive the blade home.

"No!" Mack ordered. "We just puncture the vein. There."

Barney trembled. I watched his pants quivering. Was this rage or cowardice? Mack, shouting over the rumpus made by the sacrificial beast, which he alone knew the authentic way to kill, explained the art.

"If he doesn't bleed slow, the meat won't be white. And then you'll have Mrs Murphy herself to deal with."

"Don't mess about with my pig," Mum's voice warned from the kitchen.

Barney stepped forward and let the point in through the skin. At first it wouldn't go. Then suddenly the resistance gave. Blood squirted out all down his trousers and onto his boots. He jumped back, letting the blade fall. Mack took a swipe at him but missed, and retrieved his precious knife, which he then wiped clean between finger and thumb, checking if it had suffered any damage. I rushed forward to do Ellen's job, now she was no longer needed, positioning the milk pail to catch the blood. The pig knew what was happening. He wriggled and clenched, thumping the frame the way Michael thumped his body against the bed when he had misbehaved. But the pig did not have words to curse our house of a tyrant like my brother did, nor the lovely fire of alcohol to brace him or muffle his pain in warmth.

Down along the creek, the blacks came walking, feet sprung like tall birds, till they could see the house and what was going on. I thought they must be too far off to get any clear idea, but they stayed interested, so perhaps their eyes were better than mine. Each year they heard our pig cry, but it was still new to them. Perhaps they couldn't work out why we seemed unable to kill it outright, why it had to go on crying, moaning and sobbing for ten minutes or quarter of an hour. Perhaps they couldn't even see such a simple thing as why we needed to tie the animal on a frame to do the job properly.

Barney apologized to Mack. And again I was reminded of Father Gwilym, but this time of how his voice could change in the middle of my lesson and I knew next minute his white hand would perch on my working boy's scarred brown one. Barney said it was just his clothes and the shock of spoiling them, not the blood that made him jump, no, nor, he shouted over a renewed wail from the beast facing a certainty of death, the pig yelling. "I suppose it'll wash out," he added a bit stupidly, ashamed now Ellie began to laugh at him. And even more ashamed when he found she was, more likely, laughing at the pig for making so much fuss too late to be saved.

Mum brought boiling water. She heaved the great weight of the kettle and carried it herself, out down the steps, squinting in the sunshine and steam, to set it on the bench placed ready; and then carried back the bucket of blood for cooking. This was so full that the contents tilted and some streamed down the side, landing with a soft slap in the dust, which instantly soaked it up. Mum glanced back a moment and went on her way.

The pig's cries had guttered out to a hoarse panting, and now we heard again the remote gunfire from the ocean. An eagle's shadow rippled over grass, onto the dirt, up across the pig-frame, fitting itself to the lovable plumpness of dead flesh, then away, rising the full height of a stone chimney, flickering on smoke from Mum's fire, to vanish in the blue heat of the day before the day we must all celebrate. Next time we looked across towards the creek, the Aborigines had gone. There was just a flat plate of water turning silver on its axis at the bend where one bank had collapsed in the previous year's wet.

"Look at the horses!" Kate shrieked, leaping down, prancing round the orchard and climbing an apricot tree full of Christmas apricots.

We hooted at the miserable cluster of them in the farthest corner of their yard, tails swishing the fence posts. Barney, under Mack's direction, had already begun the scalding and scraping.

"See this?" the butcher called to Ellen still at the door like a Sunday. "When you get him for a husband you ought to have him apprenticed as a butcher. He's got the feel of it, when he doesn't go throwing a man's good knives around in the dirt."

Ellen laughed. And I laughed also, at the insulting notion of a twenty-two-year-old man going for an apprentice.

As the scalding and scraping progressed, the pig's

skin gave out a rasping whistle under the blade, a persistent ghost of the sound the beast's lungs made when it was dying.

The idea had never come to me before that other animals are covered with fur, feathers, or scales but pigs go naked like ourselves. So the screams which I'd heard once a year now made me feel cold. Each Christmas past I had listened to them without realizing why our neighbours looked in during that quarter of an hour of bedlam. This particular year they included Mr and Mrs Earnshaw enjoying a drive, who waved, and the O'Donovans, cantering through the gate and far enough down the track to get a close view while young Clarrie yelled out that they'd come to check, in case you was murderin' someone! I couldn't be sure what he said at the time, but I saluted on behalf of the family, needing a part to play now Barney had cut me out of my job.

Kate in the apricot tree heard, being that much closer, and she told me a few days later, when I returned home from punching Barney in the Brian Boru, my memory hot with the loathing I saw in the eyes of men I'd known all my life, men who would not, they said, lay a finger on me if I got out right away.

I ought to say something here about my patron saint. When Pa first sent me to lessons with the nuns at the Sacred Heart Convent, he had to pay two shillings a week for my education. Though this came as a great surprise to my elder brothers, William, Michael, and Daniel, the point was not so obscure: to celebrate our little world, the family needed a historian, a law-man, a clerk, an accountant. Norah was clever enough, but because she was a girl they didn't even consider her. When I came along, I was to be it, all these things rolled into one for the sake of thrift. I had a talent for learning and for politeness, which was another reason why the priest chose me to serve at the altar and why he began taking the trouble to give me extra tuition, gratis. "Shall I tell you about your very own saint?" he asked me one day when I was still persuaded I'd become indispensable to him. Naturally I wanted to hear everything.

First he shook my faith in religion itself by explaining that Saint Patrick was an Englishman, born at Bannavem Taberniae, thought to have been near the river Severn. Such monstrous news made our world seem no more substantial than a dangling medallion, something beautiful, round and complete but too compact, too deceitfully perfect to be lifelike. When I reported this crime of Saint Patrick's to Mum, she muttered against letting that foreigner into our church in the first place. As a consequence, I found I had to fight for the right to go back to Father Gwilym the following week. I learnt a lesson from this: though Pa and Mum wanted me to have knowledge, it did not follow that I was to be at liberty to spread the muck around. My job, like a librarian's, must be to store it away so we would have it safely in the family. This knowledge might never be used, but our pride was incomplete without it. So Saint Patrick came from Britain and his parents were Christian citizens of the Roman Empire.

Accepting his word gave rise to a change in my relationship with the priest; our meetings acquired a hint of the illicit, an exciting aspect of conspiracy. The story went that the young saint was captured by Irish marauders and carried off to Ireland as their slave. You may imagine the stained-glass window of this scene in my mind: dense lines of lead, a matted confusion of ships' masts, ropes lashing the boy's hands behind his back (a boy with my own features and colouring) and his new masters dragging him off to work as a herdsman on the slope of

Slemish. Even though I was not yet fourteen, I was a herdsman myself. Since the time I began to walk, I helped with our cattle and did my share of farm work.

I began to see that Patrick *had* to be an Englishman, he had to be an outsider. Nothing ever gets done if everybody is an insider. So this was the true reason why my parents insisted I go to school; I was to be made the outsider. When he was twenty-two, my saint heard a voice promising him a mission, but he must free himself first, he must face the fact of his bondage and take action. (I myself was twenty-two in 1898, when the murders made our old life impossible to go on with and broke my father's power.)

Saint Patrick—so Father Ellis Gwilym told me in his tapestry voice of metallic glints with frayed edges round its stiff innocent pattern of words woven together as a design of facts in which each detail came forward equally with the others and nothing was relegated to background —escaped to France. There he received the call to return to the country of his enslavement and convert the Irish people to Christianity. He was consecrated as the second missionary bishop to be sent to Ireland, following the death of Saint Palladius. "The second!" I cried out, betrayed in my dream again. "Yes," Father Gwilym confirmed mildly. "There was only one who tried before him." I wondered then if Saint Palladius was an idiot like my elder brother Willie, but I didn't know how to ask such a thing. Anyway, the church portals began banging in the change of wind and I found it was almost evening, so I faced the dangers of riding the last miles home after dark, my mind filled with demons and punishments, not least of which were the actual whips of my oppressors. "It is probable," Father Gwilym had said as I left, "that Patrick, armed only with faith and knowledge, was the greatest and most successful missionary in history; within his lifetime all Ireland was his."

These were the words I said which so shocked the women; while the pig's carcase glittered with sheets of steam and the knife rasped through tough bristles and the butcher whipped thin blades along his steel and whip-birds mocked his ceremony from the surrounding bush and Mum carried the afternoon sun in a bucket of blood, I said without preamble or explanation: "Before Saint Patrick died, all Ireland was his."

Mum put down the bucket, letting its handle clunk against the metal. She withdrew into the doorway. Norah, who had come to the workroom window when the pig's cries ceased, slowly raised a hand to her throat and held it there. Ellen, on her way to soothe the terrified horses, paused to look at me questioningly, in her calm and curious way interested. Polly gave a silly shriek from indoors at the sight of blood blazing on the threshold. And Kate fell out of her apricot tree while she acted the fool, spraining her wrist which had to be bandaged, and that's how it remained (she felt an idiot, as she put it) right to the day of the funeral when not only the residents of Cuttajo and district came but, thanks to sensational items in the city newspapers, hundreds of idlers who

travelled from up and down the coast and even by Cobb
& Co. from Goulburn and Sydney. A few came from
Melbourne, over four hundred and sixty miles away. That
was how famous we became.

Cuttajo parish used to be very proud of our church in
those days. Now people couldn't care less, and the paint
has been rubbed off by sea winds. St Brigid's was built
only eight years before the murdered bodies were put in
it, yet the outside and inside had already been repainted
twice. This will give you some idea. During the building,
Pa had helped with timber, allowing volunteer pit-
sawyers into a patch of forest of ours to cut the joists and
rafters out of the straight logs he offered them. I remember it going up. I was fourteen.

The light, never too good in there, suited a funeral.
Once we were all seated and the simple coffins set regi-
mentally at the foot of the steps before the altar, Father
Gwilym made his appearance. He looked deflated, as if
he had mistaken his way, as if seeing no flowers on the
coffins caused him to doubt there was anybody inside
them, so much so that he might knock on each in turn
and not be satisfied unless he heard answers from within.
An altar boy finished setting the cruets on the credence
table for the requiem mass and knelt exactly as Father
Gwilym rose from kneeling. How many times I had done
this myself I could not count. I was thinking: Soon the
kid's knees will begin to ache and his whole mind will be
taken up begging the old fellow to finish fussing with
that chalice. When it came to the funeral service, this was

the boy who carried the jug while another held the priest's cope open so he could incense the coffins and splash holy water on them. The aromatic smoke drifted in the air, so heady it might have been a leftover from some far more ancient fertility rite.

St Brigid's was packed.

Outside, a solemn crowd of Protestants waited for their share of the pickings. At the graveyard the problem was to keep these people back. They felt they had rights and pushed close round the cortège, with their hot prickly clothes smelling of lust, hats in hand and combed heads bowed. Under their brows, cruel squids' eyes flashed and bodies dangled from their heads, feet drifting along while the firm shoulders wedged them in the best vantage point obtainable. I must have counted three hundred horses tethered to the fences on the paddock side, plus at least a hundred and fifty carriages, traps, and wagonettes. Even the bishop's landau was there. He had brought it with him when he arrived on the steampacket that morning (coincidentally with his provincial tour), though the matched grey horses belonged to the publican. His Lordship had to travel in style, I suppose, for the sake of his high office. Maybe the reason our priest shrank so badly, and the O'Donovan child clattered the sprinkling-wand in its brass jug, was simply that they knew a bishop sat, masquerading as humble, in the front pew.

At the graveside our family stood up front, hulking and immovable. Father Gwilym gave me several signs I could not interpret. He repeated them despairingly as the bishop stared at Mum, while gravediggers rescued the dead from ignominy, shovelling black soil over them, blanking them out from the impertinence of moral scavengers. I have studied fish oaring toward each other and stopping a respectful distance apart, apparently locked in some convention which will neither let them approach closer nor swim away. I felt the same, the priest's signals completely mystifying: a warning, a displeasure, a bewilderment, and an accusation. Eventually Father Gwilym produced a handkerchief and blew his nose discreetly, catching my eye above the exclamation of snowy linen. No one in our family was weeping. That was it. Only Polly, the ninny, standing apart in her lace-up boots and leaning on her husband's arm, spouting tears from a face so crinkled she looked as if she was at a music-hall and laughing fit to burst her stays. She was a McNeil now.

I found it impossible to believe the three victims would fail to turn up and join the rest of us in our amazement at the scene, the indescribable excitement, the sense of *life* all around. People half dead a week previously were out and about and vivacious with opinions and gossip.

While the funeral proceeded, public investigators were busy boiling the dead horse's head, and this very afternoon ordered the Post Office to be opened specially for them to send a telegram to Sydney headquarters conveying the information that a bullet had been extracted corresponding exactly with the cartridge case found, and adding that two good horses had been reported stolen from a farm ten miles away. EXTRAORDINARY MYSTERY ABOUT THE

WHOLE CASE, the telegram concluded. So there was. And this mystery, even more than the evidence of common bloodlust, was what enlivened the public mind.

To give you a summary: The events looked simple. The sulky had been heading back home (south) when it turned off to the left a mile and a half from Cuttajo and was driven a further half mile till it stopped at the scene. Eight witnesses saw the party on the road, seven of them also saw the other brother, Patrick (myself), on horseback at the specified times. Everyone exchanged greetings because it was a fine, clear moonlight night. There was a lot of good cheer, owing to these neighbours having been with each other at the Yandilli Races earlier in the day. Of the witnesses who saw Michael and our sisters, some also observed an unidentified man of heavy build leaning against a tree where the sliprail was. When, with her son and a friend, Mrs Carroll of the Cuttajo greengrocery met the Murphys on their way to the dance, it was just at this point. Mrs Carroll saw the man watch Michael drive the sulky past (heading north towards Cuttajo) and then walk out into the road straight for her own cart. He passed just behind, so she and her party saw him closely, but not his face, owing to his having a dark felt hat pulled down over his eyes. Her thirteen-year-old son thought it might be the new fellow employed by the butcher. Five of the eight witnesses who passed along that road during the hours 7.45 p.m. to 10 p.m. saw the stranger. Yet Sergeant Arrell, himself returning from Yandilli with a friend (whether they were drunk, as suggested, or not), had no such encounter. But not only did Miss Florence Love (who also met the sergeant on the road) see the unknown man, he approached her, passing within ten feet and muttering something she could not quite hear. Thomas Drew was quite definite that he had seen him too; and Gordon Pringle (eighteen), who passed the sliprail at 7.45 p.m., described the intruder's strong build and hat. Later that evening, others met the Murphys behaving like revellers on their return journey home. Two witnesses claimed to have heard screams in the night and shots also. Louisa Theuerkauf, at her employer's house half a mile from the sliprail on the other side of the road, having gone to bed at 9 p.m., was woken by the cats still in the kitchen at 10 p.m. (the clock struck), so she got up to put them out the back door—this door faces Earnshaws' paddock—and heard two shots, one long after the other, and two screams from the same direction repeating the word *Father, Father.* But she didn't like to wake anyone else in the house. Catherine Byrne, another resident on that western side of the road, heard screams loud at first but fading away, from the direction of Earnshaws' paddock. Such was the main evidence. The witnesses were in substantial agreement, but the facts were slight.

The overriding question in the public mind was still the one put by a reporter in the paper: How could a strong man and two healthy women be persuaded to leave the road and submit to being bound and tortured without the least sign of struggle? The tracks of the sulky with its giveaway wobbly wheel showed quite clearly that the driver did not suddenly diverge; they sloped off at an even, shallow angle, denoting a clear intention from some distance back to turn through the sliprail. Once in the paddock, all tracks were lost, while at the murder site such crowds had gathered on the hysterical advice of William McNeil and Barney Barnett, both there early, both sounding the alarm and urging witnesses down off the road, they obliterated any original footprints which the black trackers could possibly distinguish.

Had the victims, the newspapers conjectured, been killed first and then driven there to be laid out, all parallel with feet pointing west (in which case, why no blood in the vehicle?), or had they gone willingly (in which case for what purpose?), or had they been hailed and guided perhaps to rescue a hypothetical injured man (in which case, why no sign of the sulky being pulled up on the road and changing direction?), or, taking account of the fact that the killer was certainly armed, were they already being held at gunpoint while in the sulky (in which case, why were they seen so cheerful on the road minutes before the calculated time of their leaving it?)? The question remained: How could a single attacker, supposing the man in the hat were the murderer, overpower and bind three people, especially as he would need to put down his weapon to do up the bonds? Did that leave us with a gang theory? And if so, where were the other members of the gang, why had no one seen them come or go on an open road busier than any other night of the calendar? Why

was Michael's skull smashed to make it look as if he had
been murdered the same way as the girls when, in fact,
after he was exhumed seven days later, a bullet was found,
a bullet lodged in his brain, that the medical officer Dr
von Lossberg had overlooked? Could the blows of the
bludgeon, delivered with equal force to the right side of
Michael's head and the left side of each of the girls', have
been delivered by the one person? Was he ambidextrous,
changing hands for these several attacks (the angle of the
fractures betrayed the exact direction of the blows, which
could then be quite accurately reconstructed)? The puzzle
had many aspects. And finally, why was the Murphy
family so reluctant to give evidence at the inquest, or even
to see the bodies and bury them; why did they (we)
behave in a manner so markedly unorthodox as to provoke
the presiding magistrate to observe that it was as if they
(we) were holding something back?

   The magistrate asked Louisa Theuerkauf if the word
Father! which she had heard screamed might not possibly
have been *Arthur!?* Yes, she admitted, it could certainly
have been Arthur, though she had not thought of such a
thing until this moment. And Catherine Byrne also con-
ceded the voice might have screamed *Arthur!* This witness added, with some shrewdness: But whether the
screams named the person attacking or the person who
might best come to her defence against the attacker, she,
Miss Byrne, could not say, having often deliberated on
the subject of fear and prowlers, on her house being
broken into and herself assaulted.

These were puzzles. Altogether, over one hundred possible suspects were questioned by the police, and some of them detained. The ramifications welled even wider. Timber workers and shepherds reported wild men howling round their campsites wielding knives and clubs. The ironmonger did exceptional trade in new bolts and locks, also cleaning out his entire stock of ammunition. Crosses were painted on doorposts. I saw them myself and heard of cockerels secretly slaughtered for a kind of prayer dredged up from the distant superstitions of Europe and the Islands. The publican at the Brian Boru— Mr Gilbert, his name was—made a fortune out of visitors as Cuttajo earned a place on every New South Wales map printed from 1899 onwards. Our murders began to be called The Mystery. They were never solved. They still have not been solved. None of the explanations could be made to stick, not the one accusing Pa, at the upper end of the scale, nor the one accusing Sergeant Arrell at the bottom.

Yet the reason The Mystery was so widely accepted as a name had to do with more than just who might have committed the crime and how; in a religious sense, as well, it chimed with our deepest fear of life's meaning. As to the reported black magic, I'm sure I scarcely need remind you that while we speak of Australia, we also speak of Britain and the Continent. Certainly in those days most Australians had not much notion of a separate nationality, merely a separate opportunity.

In 1898 the grand imperial powers, for all the palaces

in their capital cities, the boulevards and galleries, for all
their glitter and aristocratic scepticism, were a spent force.
They lived resplendently, but the decay had eaten too
deep to be cured. The ideas going about at the time (I
mean, by this, the high ideas) quite commonly involved
a doctrine of pure blood-lines, a polite name for witch-
hunts against any intermarriage with aliens. The leaders
in this debate were nearly always weedy little chaps, having narrow chests and an asthmatic delivery, who undertook lecture tours, during which they worked themselves
into a fever on the subject of Orientals, or Slavs, Negroids,
Jews, or even Irishmen. Father Gwilym had warned me
about this. But I did not just rely on his word. I went to
the lectures and subscribed to a Travelling Library. By
1914 I was in Europe and saw for myself, being among
the first and oldest to volunteer for the Army—the AIF,
as it was called in those days. Incidentally, Artie Earnshaw
joined the same platoon. He lied about his age; he
wouldn't see forty again, that's for sure. We struck up a
new friendship and remained mates right through till his
death in 1938. We saw it all in Vienna at the end of the
war. One look at the place was enough.

But during the years leading up to this, we had no real
understanding of how we had been used, no notion that
our governments were old-boys' clubs; we only knew
that here in New South Wales people had the good sense
to resent and resist all forms of authority. That's the one
reason we escaped a full share of blame for the worst
follies in the war. If we had a virtue, this was it.

The Germans and the British had turned on each other, the Bulgarians and Russians, cousin against cousin, clan against clan, using weapons which included fear and rape as well as bullets; nothing to do with their declared motives, but all with the ferocity of a closed family for whom there is no future, no self-expression beyond carnage. When you look back on it, you say to yourself: How did it happen? such madness? such murder? the lies so senseless, so impossible to unravel, the blame so hard to assign to pardonable causes?

Is it any surprise that, in the years when these atrocities were brewing, a nation like ours thrilled to the news of a mystery at Cuttajo? No wonder people cared more for this murder and felt it reached their souls more hauntingly than any case of kindness could, or any case of heroism. The horror spoke with a million tongues. The names Cuttajo and Yandilli became instantly famous. And even Paradise was heard of in the city.

Now, after the welter of theories, none of which fitted the case convincingly, in 1956, here was that dill Barney Barnett, one-time suitor for Ellen's hand, killer of the pig, whose bloodstained trousers caused immense excitement among the investigators, hanging on to his life long enough to call an inspector of police from Sydney and make his confession.

You should have seen his face when *we* walked in as well, me and Willie and Mack followed by Jeremiah in his wheelchair and Pa on horseback. He had just begun his tale when he saw us being let through the door by the nurse. I swear it is a tribute to his strength that his heart didn't give out that moment. But he had no time to lose, intruders or not. The priest finished his preparations, mucking about with a couple of candles, setting his stole ready to put on, fussing with the tiny phial of chrism, and dropping his bottle of holy water, luckily on the bed, where the inspector himself saved it.

I watched crows flap in his eyes and points of ivory show. Poor dismal old bloke forcing out the word *marder*, as he pronounced it, and currying enough nerve to defy us, the family.

"And then I bashed the horse's brains out with the bludgeon-stick, you see."

Willie, I might mention, showed no sign of understanding, but he knew Barney well and kept giving him a poke on the foot to be recognized.

"Why?" Barney bellowed, emptily repeating the inspector's question, which might have been any number of questions and all tricky.

"This is 1956, don't you know?" he went on after a bit of dying. "I'm not talking about no bloody horse, I'm talking about him and his sisters!"

He shot a look at me, the crows flapping in there a moment to let the vision through before the priest went dabbing the lids with oil, dabbing his nostrils and his ears and mouth, and uttered the words of absolution in such a voice that you'd swear it was him about to kick the bucket.

The inspector listened, calm and polite. Mack and

Willie and I stood round with the nurse hovering behind us and the priest ready to pack his box of tricks.

"Aren't you going to write it down?" Barney whispered. "In my words?" he pleaded from lips gleaming with the blob of oil, knowing now that there was no escape from hell.

"Thank you, Mr Barnett," the inspector replied as he put his silver-trimmed cap on. "I think I have heard enough. The horse," he observed as he paused at the door, stern yet regretful, "was not bludgeoned. It was shot."

And left the fellow helpless there among us, suffering a seizure, his little nurse, daughter of Father Gwilym's best violin player, pushing us around and begging us to give him room to breathe even if we were old friends. Pa's stallion swished its clean tail and stamped one hoof. It was then, as I think I have mentioned, that the car door slammed and, a moment later, a fine pall of dust came drifting in to settle on Barney's claim to fame.

We had had the revenge we wanted.

How was an important fellow like the inspector to know that Barney's mistake did not necessarily prove he was lying? When you're humble enough, you realize the big things in life are the ones we do get wrong. They are the things which give us no rest until the brain can put its own pearly coating on them and make them bearable to live with.

After the priest, with a shrinking gesture, drew the sticky, dead lids over those subsiding wings I had seen in there, Jeremiah grumbled: "Is he finished?" being unable to manoeuvre his wheelchair close enough to be sure.

I shook my head, though he was. Then I looked at Willie, trying to guess his feelings. But he remained mesmerized by the judgment before us. Mack nodded off to sleep on his feet—you might have guessed he wouldn't last long, having no fury to keep young.

Pa had gone. He would be at home when we got back, and there he would stay, because the rest of the business concerned nobody outside the fences we had put around Paradise.

As I look back on Barney Barnett's funeral I question whether anyone can guess what love costs. Undoubtedly the cost begins in that remote babyhood predating our conscious recollections: naked mounds of warmth, a delicious skin smell, pink growths, webbed fingers (destined one day to reach adulthood perhaps by clutching the handle of some steel implement being forced into flesh), intimacies of damp hair and saliva. But isn't the cost also to be found later: while being lifted and held by some parent—the big dry warmth—who has the arrangement of the world at his or her mercy? Surely it does not just begin with that adolescent discovery of how startlingly lips move when pressed against other lips no longer quietly murmuring an anticipated lullaby; nor just with some girl called McCheyne who threw you off when you tried finding out what you were ashamed not to know; nor just with Artie's mother

hoeing her kitchen garden, presenting firm smooth forearms, capable, tender, a knob of bone at each wrist and
fine grey veins; not just with the rutting violence of
powers within yet beyond yourself, hurling your body
out of kilter, helpless to resist a monster known only by
its appetite? Who else is competent to say what love costs
a young lout unlearning, through the appeasement of
blood, the reticence and primitive rage of childhood—
exultantly feeling bones crack under his hand? Who is
to gainsay the bat-wheeling pandemonium in the brain,
or put a limit to it, or claim to know when it started or
stopped? Who am I to say I loved Ellen, or that I did not
love Norah?

This much I can tell you for certain. The sort of person
the authorities put in a magistrate's chair is he who
imagines a plain man may copulate with someone tied up
and helpless, and asks what sort of hell that would be.

The answer might be heaven, of course; as you will
know if you have ever dared refuse to be woken from the
enchantment of your free mind, from the sublime superi-
ority of your solid body achieving flight, from capitulating
to a new harmony nobody dreamed about before . . .
taking fresh gulps of it, gazing in at irises wide open as
the body's orifices to receive you, measuring your finest
minutes by her breath spurting hot against your shoulder;
while down there, in an ocean's upheaval, profounder
secrets lip you with hunger—hunger for the defeat you
bring by your self-sacrifice, the ultimate victory of the
victim, the arousal of a yearning for cruelties which are

beyond the human body's capacity to perform, until you
come to understand that the deepest insecurity lurks in
our physiological ability to receive more than we can
give . . . what then is left to do but kill? And kill for
the reason of love's ambition? Kill because of the very
power of beauty, the knowledge that to repeat such a
defeat-in-victory would make any other solution each
time less possible? Pride aches to cry out, I have crushed
your strength with my strength; I have dominated you
with such excess that the time is past when I can make do
with your fainting desire, your anger or loathing, delicious
though they are. By then love has become as desperate
as art, which must have a conclusion if it is to bring spirit
and flesh together. Pride accepts nothing less than this.
Human imagination, as I have found it, returns to the
one image of heaven it knows. The murderer does not cast
his victims away, he takes their lives into his own. Each
victim becomes wholly his. The candle gutters and dims,
and the void of helplessness has begun. For what can you
do with the body dead, the mere doll of your dominion?
Imagine, only, the virtuosity (the virtue, even) of holding off this fate, of committing your crime three times
over.

In such a case, surely only a coward would count the
compounding, the multiplication of misery to follow?
Isn't the knowledge of such hell-impending the very
mark and measure of a momentary elysium? What man
who is a man will deny his virility at the moment of dis-
charging it, by warning himself that he will be filled

with regret once it's over? And what woman would not suffer fury and insult at sensing such cowardice, such narcissism in the moment of his self-loss to her victory?

How gross, you may say, but is it more gross than accepting squalid butchery as the sole logic? Doesn't this at least allow for a fearful joy, austere in its being stripped of trivia, perfected out of the fires of doubt, simplified beyond deception? Soul to soul, flesh to flesh, pure energy? The public must sense this, or why else have they been fascinated for sixty years, savouring the horror? In relation to such an act, mere notions of right and wrong are as tuneless and as fragile as cracked plates.

Let me speak on behalf of my family. It was for this speaking that Mum sent me off to Father Ellis Gwilym during those years of study, and Pa bought a special oil-lamp (which dimmed on the night he rushed past, pursuing Willie) for me to study by. What are we old men still waiting for? I'd put it this way: the longer we (my brothers, my brother-in-law, and I) defy death, the more the guilt and the glory of those murders becomes equally shared, belongs almost impersonally to our collective clan. So you see, we do still grow! Most people will feel cheated if they are not shown a culprit—the reason being their appetite for comfort. "Not us!" they say. "So *he* was the one!" they say, fooled into believing life's tangle has been neatly unravelled for their inspection. "That's what I thought," they say, "that's human nature for you!"

Now let me make another admission. Above all, I long

to come face to face with the lovely erratic call of simply being a man who was a boy and who, after threescore years and ten, might have expected to be ready to confront his end with a philosophy of having lived as a man should through his abilities, his intelligence, his body, and his place (given or made) among his fellows. This, and not my parents' long-term foresight that the family would one day need a historian, is the reason I put my name to the present document.

I have come to see that one purpose behind our training in good and evil is so the land, this unimaginable and largely uninhabited continent, can show itself as beyond such littleness. If, like Ellen, we throw over our infantile desire to be told we are right, we're the poorer in this one respect at least, that we lose the scale of our insignificance compared to the vast country we have the preposterous nerve to call ours.

There is, do you see it, a new heroism: waiting. The old heroes went out and did battle, but our twentieth-century heroes are sufferers—the bombed, not the bombers. In my modest way I too have waited. I was a young man when the murders happened and I had a great deal to suffer before attaining strength to face what I knew, or even to see how much I did in fact know. I was still in that vanity of being at the centre of the world.

The most exciting thing in life is to be a new adult.
Just that. It is making a person for oneself. Taking who
you thought you were and creating someone as close as
possible to a person you would like to be. This risk
(whether failing or succeeding) is surely the climax of
what we know. There's no need to look further than the
realization that we can amaze our old school friends and
even our parents into having to take a decision as to
whether they like us or not. I don't believe Michael ever
achieved this. Young Johnnie at sixteen had made more
of a surprise of himself than Michael at twenty-nine.
"Hold on, John," we'd say, "what the hell do you think
you are doing?" But we were never surprised by Michael.
I know what you're thinking, that because I was seven
years his junior, this would have happened before I
knew about it. Granted, I might not have been attentive
enough as a boy to notice, but the process also shows in
the way we are treated by others. Even Mum sometimes
spoke to Johnnie with respect. Never to Michael. I
would ask you to keep in mind his childlike quality,
contemptible as well as charming, throughout this last
phase of my story.

If I must name a motive for each crime, then let it be
love, for the first murder, love for the second, and—
though more enigmatically—love again for the third.
As to an explanation of how no guilty party was ever
discovered and how the investigators made assumptions
which led them to connect the wrong things and so not

see the truth, I must take you back to Christmas Day in
that year 1898.

After lunch Ellen proposed a ramble up Blacks Creek
and into the hills, where we had seldom ventured even as
kids. Mack and Polly said that after so much pork crackling, such quantities of plum pudding and fresh cream,
they needed a snooze; Jeremiah could never be tempted,
any more than our parents; Daniel had his uniform to
think of, plus his wife's sulky mood not to be bruised;
and the young ones were already off on ponies to visit
their mates the O'Donovans, bearing a parcel of Norah's
mince pies as a gift between families. Willie said he'd
come, but then changed his mind without a reason. And
Willie was the one who stood on the verandah watching
our departure so suspiciously.

Had we planned it this way? I don't know. It's not
just that I cannot remember. I believe I didn't know at
the time either. But we could not have been better pleased
by our party, just the closest, the most affectionate:
Norah, Michael, Ellen, and myself. Yes, affectionate is
right for the tone of our general feelings, but I mean it
also to cover the fact that I guessed by this time I was in
love with Norah. Of course I did. And once admitted, I
recognized the knowledge went back a long way, even to
a dream from before puberty, a dream in which we two
lay among hay-stooks, me lolling on her naked breast.
By various other factors I can estimate my age as no more
than eight or nine. She had no idea, of course. That would

have been unthinkable. And as we set off in pairs I took care, out of a delicacy which was becoming habitual, to walk with Ellen.

Once we crossed the last of our property, the oldest paddock (called the fifteen, though I don't think it was more than twelve acres in fact), laughing as we dodged cowpats and set the flies dreaming, laughing as Michael tipped his cap at an anthill taller than himself and wished it good afternoon, laughing as he and I tramped the wire down and stretched the top wire up to let the girls through.

That had been the first paddock I ever ploughed by myself as a lad; and made the mistake of looking to Pa for a word of praise. The wound still aches through my bones, the lack of a simple gesture, even a smile. Well, once we had put Pa's kingdom behind us, we were in uncharted territory.

The bush closed round us. There were no tracks here unless they were shortcuts to a wombat hole. High trees leaned over the water and we had to fight our way through dense growths of ferns along banks thick with fallen debris which floods had thatched and stacked treacherously among the roots. Already we overreached the rule of law. When I stopped to look back, I could not see Norah our comforter . . . only a woman making a delicate gesture of alarm at how her skirts might suffer among so many snags. I turned to face my companion and share a younger person's patronizing acceptance of the slowness of those beyond the twenty-five-year limit

. . . to find, not Ellie the way I had known her, but a mature creature with unpredictable eyes, bosom already heaving inside her bodice.

We loitered on a flat bank beside the creek which, though it still flowed, showed signs of how deep the drought had grown. We were in the middle of a patch of dead reeds, the frail canes snapping as we brushed a passage through them, animal tracks impressed plainly at the water's edge, the deep sharp claw marks of kangaroos.

At the time I was struck by so slight a thing, I hesitate to mention it for fear of cluttering this account with unnecessary detail: the women held hands briefly. Though I cannot say for sure if this was done as a greeting or a parting, it certainly planted the idea in my mind that they had a compact, that even if Michael and I did not know what we were venturing into, they did.

The further we followed the creek, the further we escaped the cruel heat of that day. Deep in delicious groves of shade we picked our way. The sandy bottom with its clear ripples of glinting fish gave place to mud. Mossy rocks cluttered the banks, and logs jutted from the water among lances of light. We stood and listened to bellbirds, the marvellous density of their sound compounded of thousands of single short piercing notes, a shimmering forest of harmonics every bit as untamed as their habitat.

Trees now shut us away from the land beyond, the curtains of it drawing close on all sides. When we spoke, our voices echoed faintly. Echoes slipped off among the tattered trunks, busy as betrayers. Our laughter, though we laughed less and less frequently, took on the clanking non-expression of sounds belonging there. We came to a huge fallen tree trunk spanning the creek, solid as a bridge. A new and terrible possibility became quite clear when Michael almost rested one arm across Ellen's shoulders but withdrew the gesture as premature. Instead, he leapt up to join me on the bridge, breathing lightly and easily. He took hold of my arm and I had a memory of the girls clasping hands so little time before: just as I loved Norah, he had fallen victim to Ellie. His grip tightened, confirming that he knew I knew. Michael, famous for impulsiveness, had to keep his balance.

Till now, danger offered us a game—I had been the sole outcast among four, also the least among us if judged from the standpoint of personality. But with my brother lost to the same madness (my brother who survived his repeated defiance of Pa, my brother who would act first then think afterwards, and who had already earned a name for local amours) I recognized the thrill of our being hunters. The bush itself trembled: intense, vigilant, inhuman, swallowing us, confounding our sense of direction, teasing our ears with whispered invitations.

I thought back to the previous Christmas at the beach, when Ellen jumped into a rockpool fully clothed. How furious Michael was. I could picture Mum looking out from a cave she made of air simply by sitting wherever she sat with darkness cupped about her, watching Ellie taste salt water for the first time since she was a child, and what Ellie said about it.

Everything would be different if Jeremiah had come with us. Had he been our parents' proxy, there could be no magic, no risk. He might well cast aside his clothes, dive off the fallen tree, and plunge in the pool, throwing a chain of bright drops from his hair as he surfaced, his serious face of an animal intent on survival tilted up to reap the victory due to daring—for like the rest of us, he could not swim—water sheathing those bullish shoulders with steel.

I was glad, whatever might have been let loose, to be with Michael. Perpetually cheerful as he remained, he was the realist who wore permanent marks of an altogether different chain round his wrists, old discoloured welts. The only one not to believe in ghosts.

We reached down to help the ladies climb beside us— Norah flushed and uneasy, but Ellen thoroughly delighted, pointing where dragonflies skimmed the surface among weeds and dipped to glints of water which showed as an oily blue sheen amid the rattling stems. We listened while a frog wound up its watch during one of those unaccountable lulls in the collective glitter of bellbirds.

Children these days have so much time for play they could not imagine how any bushland as close as this remained unexplored. But then, in Queen Victoria's reign, before Federation, when New South Wales was still a colony, we worked from the moment we could sit a horse or lift a shovel. School was our leisure. We were a generation envied by our elders for having a school to go to and for learning to read. A lad with an intellectual bent was thought specially pampered if he had been allowed to put it to any use. So there we were, the four of us, excited by the unknown. We could see no sign of a home fence, no glimpse of a safe paddock beyond. We were in hostile territory. Any rules which might apply here were so alien we would scarcely have recognized them as rules at all.

At every clearing the sun blazed down, stuck at one angle. The creek bed rose steeply. Instead of broad pools of becalmed water pinned to the bottom by reed stems, here Blacks Creek fled past us through narrows, now and then presenting little basins of bubbles, spouting through fissures, flurrying among clustered stones, or twisted to coils like diagrams of human muscle. Ferns on the bank thinned as the great trees thickened and the canopy met overhead. I do not know at what stage the first change came about, but I recall hesitating, my boots skidding on wet rock, to glance back for the others (I could see the tops of their heads, the ladies with hair parted identically down the middle, giving the appearance of the same person seen twice, and Michael gallantly offering them an arm each), then scanning the forest. This was when I noticed how the land, instead of being shut away from us by riotous growth, surrounded us and swallowed us. The continent lay behind as well as ahead and on either side.

The others looked up to where I stood, their expressions instantly clouded by the same knowledge, eyes darkling violet, and their skin a wonderful texture of frail silkiness. Stubble began to show on Michael's chin; so he had not even made the effort to shave for Christmas. When I thought of the house back there, less than an hour's walk away, I could not believe anyone would recognize us again. You know how it is at those moments when you take your life in hand and steer a new course; not only do you hope your familiars will cease to recognize you, you dare not believe you will recognize them either —at least, not in anything but the unliving facsimile of a nose, a brow, and impersonal generalities such as height or hair colour. That appalling house, weighed close to the soil by Mum's unforgiving quest for release from her reiterated losses, Pa's savage fiefdom in the panoply of ground he had made productive, ground he had scourged of the spirit of those who inhabited it while our folk were paddling coracles at the outer fringes of some bog, cogitating an idea that if the mud could be dried it might be made to catch fire and burn with however surly a heat, folk domesticated in the service of some sickle-wielding dumbshow paganism we had risen to after we saw no future in human sacrifice, or at least after we grew sceptical of butchering selected victims one at a time, and chose the more democratic and wasteful system known as war.

That appalling house held shades scarcely more credible than Mum and Pa: Willie haunting the windows, casting fearful, slow, cunning glances round the verandah, hands clenching and unclenching like valves necessary to

the operation of his thinking mechanisms; Jeremiah en-
throned in flesh sufficient to be its own warrant, biding
its time and content to remain apprentice for some years
longer to a trade of tyranny about which he still had
much to learn; Polly and her butcher snoring porky
satisfactions in neighbouring rooms, a perfect match in
subtlety of mind. The Christmas heat pressed in as sky;
the wall-less house taken over and subdued.

We had trespassed outside our fence, yet the continent
took us to its cool recesses as holiday adventurers. We
men rolled up our sleeves. The women gathered skirts
clear of undergrowth. In an obsession to reach somewhere unknown, we had lost the power of speech. This
was the odd thing: we were now in a hurry. Scrambling
and leaping, pressing ahead through the gully's dense
vegetation. Some powerful urgency drove us, or rather
drew us, until we shed all sense of effort and, instead of
pushing on higher, seemed to be standing still while the
land itself slid towards us complete with timbers and
thickets, the creek foaming free at twice its speed, birds
gathering close in deafening excitement over our intrusion. The foliage fluttered with eyes and fingers, a
flicker of white feathers, a dash of ochre paint, whole
trees gliding by and ridges of veined rock gliding too. A
columned ravine opened ahead, swinging wide and already painfully bright; its rugged line of cliffs etched
harsh repetitions of pulsing light in the eye. Behind our
heads leaves dangled sharp as knives, honed blades chim-
ing faintly and multitudinously. A foreign odour lingered

as a tidemark in the atmosphere, an odour so foreign it roused ancient memories of numberless forebears, a collective awe, an inherited taboo, moveless as ourselves while that hinterland swept to engulf us in so vast, so unsoilable an innocence no name would do for it. We stood in a drifting grove of macrozamia palms which had most probably been alive when Captain James Cook first sighted the land, and even a hundred years earlier, when Dutch traders quit these shores as unlikely to offer any treasure worth taking; alive when King Henry VIII outraged all credulity by naming himself head of the Church for a whole nation despite every article of believable faith—yes, that is how ancient these stumpy tufted trees were, these same individuals, being among the longest-living things on earth, elders of all plant life and animal life, now alert as a committee around us, passing in review, fans of leaf sprouting elegant headdresses, a convocation of weirds, hiving their huge phallic seedcases which would break apart on ripening raw red, rot and collapse in the hope of tempting flocks of pterodactyls to feast at them, to come gliding on leather wings beneath the spotted-gum canopy, wheeling, settling, crocodile jaws busy and ponderous lizard bodies shuffling over bark-mulch, feasting right to the foot of two tall rocks which stopped the heart, rocks solid like our parents yet a hundred times bigger, brooding moss-grown judgments, heavy as the moon, knowing as the heart. So unexpectedly they loomed over us, all courage drained from my body.

At the foot of these rocks a broad flat stone was disfigured by smears of blood where patterns had been painted in yellow and orange clay.

The blood lay, as still as our amazement, drying around the edges but quite fresh, each splash isolated, anguished like a marine creature in some killing element, cast up by a vanished sea and left to die of air and warmth. The whole idea of sacrifice has always been that the killers may live longer and more prosperously under a malign despotism of powers whose vastness necessarily sets them beyond comprehension, beyond such errors of scale as virtue and vice.

The bellbirds had fallen silent. Rushing leaves now hovered, still and deadly; the creek carried jagged shards of sky down into the gully out of sight, witnessing the way we had come. The beating of air, still thudding on the inner ear, became an answer to our hearts. We were surrounded. The whole bush alive with mouths and hands, with flowers and twigs stuck on to living shadows in patterns dictated by ancestors, dead long ages ago, but gathered perpetually at that arena to oversee the ritual and assuage their innate fury of the disembodied.

Under our boots the lichened stone lay long and flat as a tongue. This was the estranged world, the world we call grotesque because, though we may have forgotten its forms, we have not outgrown our fear of it. The ravine's emptiness was what gave that spilled blood its peculiar power.

Astonishing to think our peaceful creek, from which we drew water for ourselves and our cattle, rose in such wild springs.

I had reached my province. As altar boy, school dux, special pupil of the learned Father Ellis Gwilym, assistant to the Sisters at the Sacred Heart Convent, and the only one beloved of our mother, my training led me to this moment: Michael was in my power, Norah too, and even Ellen (if only for reasons of inquisitiveness). Clearing the new paddock, burning trees, defeating Barney, and watching the pig slaughtered . . . all fell into place as the prelude to a revelation flickering round me in spears of light, the cliff line bonily gauzy as an insect wing, earth heaving its segmented body, hundred-celled eyes turning upon us as we stood where human blood had already been spilled.

The Holy Spirit spoke in whispered syllables so protracted and dreamlike I could not tell what they said, though I knew their meaning. I was shown the vanity of those destined to die with a mission; the vanity, in other words, of being one among the damned, the supreme opportunity for making my claim on God's personal wrath. Think of that, a sublime glory second only to the glory of claiming His personal love, which is the exclusive lot of the saints in paradise.

Norah had already rushed back the way we came, panic betrayed in the loose flutter of her sash, the wide-flung despair of those pale handsome arms, and Michael leaping after her.

They were gone. The Holy Spirit whispered. Heart-
beats of Its malignancy or benevolence (who is to dare
judge?) throbbed closer. Ellen watched me, maybe expecting me to speak, and then stooped down. I could not
have guessed what she was about to do. Gathering her
skirt in one hand, she reached out with the other, this
girl who was not even afraid of Pa and had yet to be
taught the imperative of morality, and placed a finger in
the congealing blood. She shot me a challenging look,
paused a moment for my reaction, and then studied her
finger. We were joined by our listening to the sound of
Norah's flight and Michael's pursuit: we heard a branch
crack, we heard her utter a stifled shriek, we heard his
voice soothe her with words as impossible to interpret
as the pulse of air. Then, like a naughty child, Ellen licked
the finger clean. She even held it up to show me: See?
All gone! . . . that finger, shiny with saliva, such a slender
girl's finger, held the way we tested the direction of the
wind. The hot afternoon gushed about us, woken again
to a swirl of birdcries, a cacophony af screeching and
tinkling.

"No harm done" was all I could think to say.

If I then took hold of Ellen, took her in my arms,
wasn't it to save her by my own sacrifice? Wasn't it with
full knowledge of ambush? Hadn't I watched the whole
scenario of *Caught Unawares*? Trees tossed wild heads
above us while the undergrowth flashed and flickered. I
shielded my sister from the consequences of her sacrilege.
I understood that I could never, now, go home to Paradise.

In those days, you see, we had no books to tell us what was expected of a man. All we knew, from Pa's readings, was how the saints behaved. There was no cinema to show us the body's language of love, however falsified a version it might be. We had never even seen a man and woman kiss, except as a greeting or a farewell, and then rarely— because who went away? My doubts concerning myself were absolute. We knew a terrible lot about God's program for punishing us if we did begin to sin seriously, but nothing at all about how to incur this punishment. Those of us who went to school had heard plenty in the playground, and believed most of it. Yet some deep sense of self-preservation warned me that this was not the authentic evil, this was hysteria, this was nothing more than the salaciousness of those who were too young to know. So, in our ignorance, Ellen and I held each other.

"In England," Father Gwilym once told me, "Saint Brigid is known as Saint Bride."

Far below, where the creek reappeared to glide from one placid sandy pool, already violated by our footprints, to another, sunshine rippling over its clean gravel bed, Michael and Norah emerged. They had dwindled to tiny figures in ridiculously white clothing, with ridiculously pale doll-limbs. They paused to see if they could make out what we were doing. They stood gazing back up to where we vacillated at the high lip of the ravine. They shaded their eyes as they stared straight into the sun to look for us.

I do not know why Michael got so drunk that night. He filled the house with laughter. While Pa was trying to beat some decorum into him, he laughed. Once or twice during the night, even, chained to the foot of the master bed, he rattled the frame that held them (Mum and Pa) together, and let slip a further chuckle. I was awake to hear, being held to account by Jeremiah, the only one still true to the faith of the house, dropping his rough clothes on my bedroom floor, displaying himself to rob me, with the sure instinct of an inquisitor, of such power as I had found in myself that Christmas Day.

You see, I did go home, after all.

The one thing I cannot explain is why I carried my revolver on Boxing Day. I understand my brothers and sisters perfectly well. The puzzle is myself. Willie's suspicions were obvious, even though I had not then glimpsed the possibility of his subterfuge, the complexity of his revenge against authority. Just as clear were Barney Barnett's reasons for jealousy. We had no idea either of them might be present, of course, any more than they suspected one another. But my own fatal whim to carry the .38 is simply beyond divination, an inspired stupidity, a genuine touch of providential will, perhaps. (Again, the vanity of the damned!)

Well, having come to the day of the crime, let me repeat that while we were still at the Yandilli Races, Ellen asked who would escort her to Cuttajo for the traditional dance: "Michael?" she suggested straight off, as if he were on her mind. And she looked past me to make clear that our moment of closeness the previous afternoon gave me no special rights. As for him, he didn't take to having it put like that. He was still sore, I suppose. His wrists and neck rubbed raw, so I don't imagine he relished wearing a collar. But Norah put him in his place: "You make too much of your own feelings." And instructed him not to treat Ellen as a child still: "She is a woman and we ought not to forget it."

Norah's strictness with him reminded me of a youthful dream . . . the virgin in a walled garden had Norah's face, just as the pale naked unicorn she nursed in her lap had mine. *Paradise* began life as a Persian word for *garden*. In this tapestry the walls were high and the enclosure crowded with flowers and the knowledge of prohibitions itself went to our heads like perfume.

1898 was among the driest years on record, as I remember. We felt the drought even in our damp corner of the country. Grass, having been parched brown by the sun, was then nibbled to its roots. Bleached earth crumbled under the hoof. That track we had cleared to the new creek helped our animals, but they were still desperately short of feed and in dire condition. The whole district lived on edge with worry. Yet at Christmas the weather played strange tricks. Night showers lasting twenty seconds shed enough moisture to rest on the dusty ground, lighter than insect eggs, through the cool snap of dawn, to rise again and float up in a mist as fugitive and sterile as a mirage.

When we four parted that evening, I on my way

homewards and they on their way to the dance, I expected
the sulky to return soon. Naturally I did. Hadn't I looked
in at the hall, spoken to the violin band, and seen failure
already stamped across the occasion? Either they declined
to believe me when I reported this or Michael had planned
an excuse for getting the girls home late. As a fallback
we arranged to meet in Earnshaws' bottom paddock, because the stock had been moved only a week before and
the place stood empty. We said we might conduct our own
private dance, just two couples, a celebration as exclusive
as it was illicit, a climax to the previous day's disturbing
events. And when would another opportunity arise for
discussing the urgent things we needed to say? I think I
might reasonably claim that the others (Norah and
Michael, if not Ellie, never Ellie) felt as confused and
guilty as I did myself, as lost in the labyrinth, as anxious
to be comforted. I only question whether they would have
stayed in town had the dance been on. I'm doubtful.

Don't you see how it always is? Once we reach the
very boundary of our known world and its morals, when
we look, as our Lord once did, over a vast plain filled
with possibilities of life and riches, *then* the Devil tempts
us. If you think that my first surrender on a ceremonial
rock high above a native gully (innocent enough in the
light of what followed) would have shaken me to my
senses, sounding such alarms the whole of Christendom
might hear and condemn, then you know nothing of
such matters. Up till the moment I reached this forbidden border, I could find strength to endure the part-

life I had come to accommodate comfortably enough.
Yet from the moment I turned my gaze outward, nothing
would satisfy me but total ruin.

The moon being bright we went for a walk by the
sea, Norah and I. Earnshaws' fence in those days ran
right along the cliff top. We stood witnessing the rise
and collapse of dazzling waves as meaningless, as un-
limited, as restless and spiritual as the land we had
ventured into the previous afternoon. I wanted it this
way: my mind a clear space in a safe cavity. At last I
realized why I had brought the gun. Truly the plan had
been subconscious and struck me as inspired.

If I took the lead, this was thanks to my liturgical
education and being the one schooled in how irrevocably
we were damned. The last remnant possibility of purity
would be judged by the coinage in which we might pay
at the end of this horror. I determined to seize the opportunity of having the matter out in the open between
us and visualized myself, not just with Norah, but with
Michael and Ellie too, calming their distress and solving
the enigma: we should put an end to each other's lives,
cleanly, quickly and, yes, lovingly. But as it fell out, I
could not wait until we got back to where we had spread
a blanket for us all to sit down together. I became possessed by a mad desire to shine in Norah's eyes.

"I am going to shoot myself," I told her.

That was how I proposed we should make love.
Suicide was the wound she must save me from. She must
save me also from hollow impotence, from the inade-

quacies I suffered as a consequence of Jeremiah's claims on power the previous night. Only she, she as a woman, could restore me.

Doubtless you will say that, had Norah not been willing to do it anyway, no threat on earth would have persuaded her. But I don't believe this does justice to her dedication to healing. Afterwards, of course, the gun presented quite different possibilities. We did not have to speak of our intense joy, or of the certain fate we had invited into our lives. I repeated the same thing in its new context.

"I am going to shoot myself, Norah."

My feeling at the time was certainty, an inspired certainty that she would beg me to release her and shoot her first. She just nodded slowly. But not for me, I sensed, for herself somehow. Slight as it was, that exclusion of my feelings, of my love for her which burned more horribly than ever, shocked me into reconsidering. It was as clear as this: Did she, to put it vulgarly, want me out of the way? We had not spoken about love. We had not spoken about anything yet, this was the strange part. Norah, adopting her entrenched protective role, simply put out her hand for the weapon. What was I to do? The old craven Patrick, Mum's favourite, succumbed. Almost as unaccountable as my having brought it in the first place, I delivered the revolver into her keeping.

"It's warm!" she objected with surprise (surely not distaste?).

"I put two cartridges in," I explained and let my ex-

planation hang, because a suicide who means business
does not need two. Also because I then knew I had never
intended to include Michael or Ellen.

Suddenly she was running. That's all I know. Taking
me completely by surprise, Norah ran and stumbled. My
heart leapt into my mouth; I thought she might fall and
the weapon go off, the cliff being pocked with a warren
of rabbit holes. She almost went down, but the force
driving her would not permit it. This must certainly have
been the same force holding me in check. Aware that I
ought to give chase, I made no move. The sensation came
close to being the most profoundly gratifying I have at-
tained, that lassitude in the face of disaster. Once she was
out of sight I was released from the charm. I ran after
her, dodging among shrubs and wattles till I came out at
the corner of the open paddock.

The flash of the revolver gave a dull angry gleam to
what was already perfectly clear. My horse trotted off
toward the gate, the other horse whinnied and stamped
and shook itself still. The sulky's shafts creaked.

Michael and Ellen, still clothed, had been so engrossed
in one another they neither saw nor heard anyone approach. Let me repeat: there was a saintly patience and
precision about Norah, even in this act of holding herself
in check till she stood right over them before squeezing
the trigger. We all knew how to use a shotgun, which
goes without saying to anyone brought up in the bush,
but I don't suppose she had ever handled a revolver before.
Her flesh felt chilled when I took the .38 from her. She

offered little resistance. There had been no shout, no scream, not a word exchanged that I could hear; the echo of the shot drowned any noise my brother's body might have uttered in shock. Suddenly I knew the Spirit was still with us, the watching beast of our expedition the previous day, a presence now akin to a mountain of stilled air.

I put the revolver in the sulky for safety and then returned to where my sisters knelt on the blanket, re-dressing Michael's clothes, using the hems of their skirts to wipe him clean, and fastening his buttons. They rolled him on his side with the wound upwards as being, per-haps, the most neutral, the most natural position in this wholly unnatural circumstance. He looked pale as putty. His head lagged and lolled horribly. The task became a matter of efficiency, a familiar challenge to achieve results beyond criticism, beyond punishment, in which we had been professionals since childhood.

Still no one spoke, but I drew closer to Ellie. She and I must protect our Norah. Michael, having died the instant the bullet pierced his brain, was beyond help. As yet we hadn't room for grief. Shock simply wiped out whole areas of the mind, to isolate the immediate scene and clear the issue of any clutter which might reduce our efficiency at securing Norah's safety from the law. Norah herself felt it; she took a modest part in the work, accepting the station of an assistant, prompt in her anticipation of what might be needful, always following, always humble. Right from the decisive moment when she relinquished my weapon she acted with gratitude for our quietness of duty.

In the looks we exchanged by moonlight we acknowledged that no simple comfort could be sought. Everyone at home would still be up: Mack, Danny, and Jeremiah playing cards, the women preparing supper, Pa reading a sentence an hour from *Lives of the Saints* . . . no, we could not return without Michael or the blanket, hoping Norah and Ellie might talk their way (or even mine) out of a murder charge. They had to be armed with an alibi so convincing not even a court of law would question it.

Once the decision had been taken and I had tied them up, using a sash and handkerchiefs, I had the idea that I ought to drive them closer to the road and leave them at a spot from which they would never have been able to witness the murder. Too late to untie them, I'd have to hoist them into the sulky. But they did not seem to mind this idea when I put the new plan in that hasty, hushed voice of a conspiracy. They lay on the soil, mute with terror and guilt. I cannot tell you what delusions of masterfulness surged through me at this time as I turned on my heel to go to bring the sulky closer. Beside the horse stood Willie. His hand caressed its neck, gentling, wooing the beast not to give him away.

Willie, solid and arrogant in one of Pa's hats (the hat identified by the old man at the inquest as his), was not the Willie we had come to expect. He aimed my revolver at me. That was what I saw in the clear moonlight on the night of the cancelled dance, when already I was expected home from work. Willie, like a child, transformed by importance in the moment he chose.

How shall I put it, the way he stood? His gesture became crucial. There was, in the standing, a certain triumph which could have no other cause than that he had seen, and therefore was judge of, our crimes. His tilted hips, the squared shoulders, the head cocked for listening to a private catalogue of what he now held in memory to empower him to ride over our superiorities, made clear he knew Michael and Ellen had broken the law, human as well as divine. Neither was it impossible that he knew about Norah and me. Certainly he had seen my darling Norah shoot the brother she was closest to (yes, this is the bitter truth it has taken me a lifetime to face). He knew the three of us planned to conceal the murder. Behind that steady barrel, aimed unflinchingly at me, stood a suppressed fury we none of us had taken seriously. This stocky man already approaching middle age was the one who paid the price of partial liberty for us all; only to see us end up in the clutches of vice. You knew how little he had to look forward to. For some years now, William had been going bald. He took shelter in a mortified slyness from such evidence of his life having already been laid waste. He became more like a retarded uncle than one of our generation. We could not forget that he had done nothing to earn this partial death except wish to leave home. And now Willie knew, by whatever intuitive faculty, that so long as he kept silent about the crime, he could exact the same payment from our freedom as Pa had claimed from his. Somewhere in those dim disoriented relics of a brave mind he claimed us as his creatures. He saw this and—guilt being an especially swift and acute aspect of the intelligence—so did we.

Some terrible alarm began ringing in my brain: Michael is dead. But I could not rise to the consciousness of it.

"This is a matter for Pa," I said in a tone of reassurance. And they were the only words spoken since the tender things I'd offered Norah, including a proposal of dying together.

I began to walk towards William, my hand held out for the .38, eyes fixed on the brim-shadow where his were hidden. Slow as a snake I moved, not even sparing a glance for the girls. This new Willie, if he was capable of lying in wait and storing his evidence without once crying out in horror or compassion or even jealousy, might also be capable of firing at me. Nor was I free from the hope that he might, because then he could not shoot Norah. He made no move as I went gliding closer. Calm as the big spotted-gum trunk he stood beside, that tree with a rotten socket about twenty feet up where a branch had once broken off and fallen, long since decayed to mould underfoot and powdered to dust in the drought we were suffering, Willie waited.

The appalling scream from behind me, followed by other, longer-drawn and more despairing screams, locked me in mid-step. Surely the revolver had not gone off? I saw no flash. William never flinched or changed aim. Pa's hat sat as a solid block against the dry silvered backdrop. The horse whinnied again and again, rearing up as far as the sulky would allow, lashing his hooves.

To this day, I marvel at it: not only did my brother find the resourcefulness to catch us out and keep hidden from sight till he could be certain we were his captives, but he must also have seen, past my advancing hand, past my shoulder, past the dead body on the blanket, past Norah and Ellen (who had now stood, leaning together for sheer human survival, wrists and ankles bound by satin and linen, invested with helplessness as a plea before the full fury of the law, tottering poles of women bedecked for some pagan festivity), the wild appearance of Ellen's fiancé wielding a length of timber.

Abandoning myself to William's mercy, I spun round to find Barney Barnett victorious above a huddle of fallen clothes. Norah, still drawing out her scream to a length of shining silk from as far back in human history as treachery was known, a slender banner more hideous than any parasite, turned the gape of her shock to me. She had become unrecognizable.

"Now," said Barney, who sounded a bit shaken, reaching to grasp Norah's bound arm but addressing us men, "it's her and it's me as well. You have to keep the secret for both our sakes."

Norah's loathing as she realized what he meant knotted her body in a spasm of nausea and wrenched her free of his grip. How shall I convey that pitiful sight, her attempt to edge her way towards the cover of the nearest tree? You must remember her feet were clamped tightly together by the binding I myself had tied. She worked her dancing pumps sideways, miraculous in her balance as she was tragic, tall as she was vulnerable, her objective transparent as it was useless. Simply put, Norah's instinct drove her, I suppose, to do something, however inadequate; the very effortfulness of her escape being a blaze of defiance against that calm elation said to be felt by victims of tradition, whose cultural role in a ritual greater than the sum total of its celebrants may represent the triumph over self.

William held still, a judge-figure and revenger before whom any squalor of human passions and fallibilities was destined to be played out beyond all compromise or mercy. He did not fire when I sprang at Barnett. He must have watched me (was it with a family satisfaction?) as I caught the club swung at my head, wrested it from the murderer's hands, threw it aside, and began punishing him. I did not want to knock him out, as I was fated to on the following day at the Brian Boru, because I intended to hurt him. But I had not long been working on him, standing over his doubled-up form, smacking at the side of his head with my fist (as much as to say: Chin up, man) while forcing his arm to tortured angles, when he let out the wild howl of a trapped scavenger.

The horse, already moon-eyed and scared out of its wits, reared in the shafts. I looked back to see it high and dangerous above Pa's hat. William shot the animal on the spot, peremptory as his dignity of office required, and no further disturbance to be tolerated. Bang . . . order had been restored. Night poured into its night shape. Yet it was Norah's whispered words rather than the shot which paralyzed me so I let my victim go.

"I can't stand any more of this."

I don't believe Willie heard, although the frogs and crickets had been shocked dumb and even the ocean confined itself to hushing among rocks. Still, he let Barney creep away, which proved to be the cleverest tactic of all. That cowardly form diminishing through undergrowth beyond the fence, as I have thought about it since, allowed free, kept open the possibility of our family surviving. Willie may not have heard, no, but he himself did speak.

"You better be careful, Pat, or you're in trouble."

This was when Norah turned on me, her manner almost as brutal as scorn. Of all the consequences which might have arisen from the maze we blundered into the previous afternoon (memories of dead reeds snapping, the deeply incised claw marks in sand, of blood spilt and outraged invisible presences, the beast unfurling its stony gauze wings, earth shifting as a segmented body, of Ellen's wild heat nestled against my own wildness, of Jeremiah naked, of our casual charade at the picnic races and my horse going lame on the way), one thing I had never imagined possible was Norah's hatred.

I set my back to Willie now, for I knew what he could not know: that he had no more cartridges left. He went on aiming at me, I presume. I had no fear of him unarmed. Nothing but pity. And for the moment, this pity was overridden by the pain Norah's words caused me.

"Him?" she cried in a fury as she stood wavering, still bound hand and foot according to our rescue plan to save her paying for Michael's murder. "He's got no trouble, no, except that he raped me, William. Raped me! Do you hear?"

I have referred before to the curious action of shock in protecting an emergency part of the brain from unwanted information. I, as a man able to defend myself against Barnett armed with his club, against my elder brother regardless of what he might be doing behind my back, stood helpless under these few words, unmanned by a feeling of futility. They severed me utterly from everything I treasured, the simple fantasies and security of a world experienced freshly as *the* world. Unmanned also by a philosophical exhaustion, by so grand a panorama of the ideas which have shaped history that neither one nor another can claim more than to have been, and to have been noted. The power of what was being played out in this tragedy went so far beyond me that I had acted as a mere instrument in the conflict without waking up to the fact that I was never my own master in any sense. I don't mean this phrase *in any sense* for an excuse or to claim the rights of either helplessness or irresponsibility. I mean that, strongly as I fought, agonizingly as I felt, vainly as I believed I was appointed to civilize my family, in those moments I came face to face with my

insignificance. What had I done, after all, but commit a
mortal sin, knowingly defied the millennia of warnings,
dressed my surrender in the motley of free will, even of
justifiable revenge against oppression . . . as if there were
not a whole world of possibilities beyond the Paradise
fences, or means enough to escape for a person who
already travelled nine and a half miles a day to work at
the convent and nine and a half miles home. Shame
robbed me of strength. I could not oppose her. Much
later I came to wonder whether this might have been
the exact opposite of the effect Norah hoped her accusation would provoke. But if so, any shortfall in my fury
when exposed and denounced was adequately taken up
by William.

I have noticed that once we are off our stroke, blow
after blow may be struck, and we seem unable to do more
than stagger back to our feet and wait, only capable of
gathering wits enough to be aware we are once again too
late to ward off a well-aimed attack; only capable of
lurching from some absurd mishap to a second and a third.
Barney armed with a bludgeon was one thing; Willie,
similarly armed, quite another, witless as he was.

Fatally, as I saw him rush at us, I presumed *I* was to
be my brother's victim. And who would not find excuses
for him, driven to the madness of nemesis, dedicated
wholly to destroying the destroyer of whatever honour
our family might have salvaged from this crime? It was
not vanity that flung me aside to dodge the anticipated
blow, far from it—nor even a symptom of self-importance

—it was the instinct for survival. But by doing so, I lost the chance of regaining my balance once I saw my mistake. Willie's victim was not me at all. He was after Norah. Ankles tied to prevent her running and wrists bound behind her back, her submission rendered extraordinarily touching, this was a Norah transformed anew: just as fury against me had shocked her out of any semblance of generosity, now her peace appeared to be instantly restored. Of course she, also, must have expected I was the one Willie would attack. Only at the last fragment of her suffering did she recognize the relief she craved. The look she turned on him as he swung his club in one hand (the left, because he was left-handed), and brought it down on her skull with crushing impact, was what I had hoped for myself: love.

At Barney's own funeral there was no visiting bishop, nor a senior police officer with silver laurels on his cap, and not even Pa. Pa had finished with him. But I sat in the church thinking things over.

This was not the old church Pa helped build, but a cold brick box with Byzantine pretensions. The new generation of O'Donovans had faithfully produced yet another altar boy. An electric organ bleated and the priest bleated too. Then I noticed to my astonishment that the child, so clumsily rattling the wand in the brass jug, appeared to be crying. There was an explanation. Barney's daughter, who died the previous year in a car crash, had married Gary O'Donovan, and this was their son. What would the boy think, I wondered, if he knew his grandpa had murdered my sister Ellen and claimed to have committed two other murders as well? How ruthless the dying are in their thwarted ambitions. Suppose Barney's bid for notoriety did convince the inspector—wouldn't this little chap be hiding at home now and facing a life of ostracism, real or imagined?

Our Cuttajo congregation muttered responses. A wind from the sea smelled of loss and damp rope. The salty autumn daylight crept in at the open portal. Blots of muddied sunshine splashed across the aisle from sightless orange windows.

Maybe Barney was more cunning than we gave him credit for. It's not impossible that he thought he would trap us into a giveaway objection when he claimed sole credit for baffling everyone. This way, in the act of escaping by natural death, he'd have enjoyed the satisfaction of knowing we must face ruin.

Was it possible, on the other hand, that the scavenger intended his deathbed confession as a kindness? With Willie and me both present, his taking the entire blame on himself might have let us off; might have been to acknowledge that, but for him, Ellen and Norah would in all probability still be alive. Did he also suspect that if Ellie were bethothed to any suitor other than himself, she mayn't have yielded to Michael's lust? Whatever the case, I'm glad I was too old to be called on as a pallbearer.

Mack, kneeling beside me, suddenly leaned nearer.

"It's for God to strike the blow!" he hissed in his deaf man's whisper; then he leaned the other way to Jeremiah's wheelchair and added, grunting as he stood up long after the rest of us: "Before they stick him underground."

But I was infuriated by the possibility that Barney might have been trying to take it upon himself to save us, to gain power over us, and defeat us by presuming to be our protector. I swore then that I would begin writing this history as soon as I returned home.

It remains only for me to explain that when I smashed Michael's head in, I used both hands on the haft of the weapon, as Barney had done, to strike an identical wound. How could I have brought myself to do it, you ask, even though he was dead? Well, I did not think of the plan right away. First I got Willie, who had been drained of wrath and left more lumpish, more witless after his brief mastery than before, to help give me a leg up the tree. Having reached the hole about twenty feet above, I found, as experience of timber had taught me to expect, the trunk was piped and at least partly hollow. I dropped the revolver in and heard it clunk down safely inside. With my free hand I sorted about in my pocket for the empty cartridge shell I had picked up from where Norah fired at Michael. I cursed myelf for not having carried it in my teeth, and retrieved it only by turning the complete pocket inside out. I dropped the cartridge in the hole, to be lost forever with the weapon, then jumped down and asked Willie to fetch my horse—which had strayed to the far fence, such an impassive creature it was, at the shots and screams. He seemed grateful to have someone else take on the burden of thinking. In this nightmare of lost bearings, I could only cling to small practical things, all else threatened me with formless horror as a wild hinterland of violence and meaninglessness.

Ellen had fallen near Michael. Whether from some trivial motive or a devious foresight, I lifted her and placed her body beside his on the blanket. My reasons are beyond me to reconstruct. But yielding to squeamishness, I positioned them back to back. I remember doing that and thinking of what I was doing too. The good side of her head looked familiar still.

Willie brought my horse and stood with it near the dead one, his whole demeanour begging to be told what this was about. How could I hand him over to the law? The less so as he certainly knew the secret of my crime of tenderness. But to save him meant saving Barney too, which explained the expression enlivening Barney's face as I let him go—the artless smirk of a player who holds the joker in his hand while others must calculate each move with their utmost (futile) skill.

The torn edges of Michael's wound, that hole blasted in his temple, bright even by the ruthless moonlight, gave me an idea: what if our best alibi were already in existence, already active in the public mind? I will explain in a moment.

I instructed Willie to pick up Pa's hat, which had fallen unheeded at some stage, and dust it so Pa wouldn't know. Then sent him off home by his own way. He possessed whatever cunning was needed for this completion of his plan, whether he intended the carnage he caused or not. As he went, my horse snuffled closer to where the corpses lay, groping for grass though Earnshaws' cattle had bitten it down to the roots. I noticed she had gone lame again in the same leg she hurt when Jeremiah raced her that morning on our way to Yandilli. By the time I set out for work at the convent the injury had looked better. But here she was, favouring the foot. While her main attention remained on the chance of feed, her hoof felt for the ground as tenderly as a lesser creature with a shrinking mind of its own. Well, now I had an alibi! Plus a reason for walking home and avoiding, as far as practical, the stony road.

Piece by piece, the horror shaped itself in my mind to something absolutely unforeseen: crime. The word *alibi* switched on a light. This was a crime. A crime big enough to have the whole shire fascinated. Yes. The fascination would reach deeper than horror.

I aligned each corpse, head towards the rising sun.

Calm, like an aspect of the weather, I viewed the scene. I have never thought more clearly, or felt more intensely necessary to Pa's kingdom. This was to be my expiation for those I loved who lay dead. They would be made famous by the same stroke that would save Willie and the rest of us. One adjustment to the facts (I sensed this rather than asserting it)—one, or two at most—might raise the crude brutality of evidence to the realm of the inexplicable.

Michael was the key, there could be no doubt, Michael, who had not been bound as the girls had, but who bore the weals of his humiliation on Christmas night. All I needed to do was supply the missing bonds. I recalled one handrail on the old sulky having worked loose even before the wheel was knocked awry, and that I had stopped the rattling by a temporary measure, warping it and tying it with some cord left over from Mum's clothesline. The cord was still there. So this is what I used, fitted to the fresh welts. Essentially The Mystery was set up. By making all three of them helpless as victims, it would be implicit that they had suffered at the hands of the same killer or band of killers. Nobody would think of accusing any one of *them* of murdering another. And, perhaps even more importantly, nobody would suspect the girls' deaths had begun with love. Without doubt it would be construed as rape in both cases: most likely by the same assailant. And mightn't such an assumption be reinforced when it was found that the identical lump of wood had been used to kill them? There was no doubt in my mind: the use of this weapon would be taken for the murderer's signature. So I disguised my brother's fatal bullet wound—as I have already explained—with a similar blow.

You must understand something else about my state of mind, as I now think back on it. At the instant I had

seized my chance to surrender to the supreme pleasure
(what a word for the stringency of love!), I accepted
that its brief release could never be repeated. Norah, incapable of consciously sinning, would not fall twice; I
believe I knew this, though I had no way of foreseeing
the means by which she might seek to elude temptation.
I have come to accept that what made it so complete a ful-
fillment was my rashness, the fact that I wittingly sacri-
ficed the remainder of my life in return for a momentary
escape. Well, nothing could be precious to me again, you
see. Somewhere in the back of my mind I felt I had a
right to punishment. It was my inheritance. And I needed
to live in order to suffer it as fully as could be. For the
sake of this suffering, I must avoid the immediate danger
of being convicted for what I had not done (the murders), so that I might be truly convicted for what I had
done.

I worked at fever pitch, as if rehearsed in each detail.
To answer the question: How did I bring myself to do it?
I shall reply: Inspiration.

Mind you, this was a very different matter from the
nausea I felt when, just as I had checked everything,
smoothed such footprints as were visible at night, attended to the details of leaving nothing incriminating,
nothing to connect the crime with William or Barney, I
thought to provide the girls too with a second death such
as Michael had. Quite like a surgeon, I removed the hame
strap from the dead horse and slipped it round Norah's
neck. Why Noah first? I bent above her, suddenly over-

whelmed with the intimacy of what I was doing. I became dreadfully ill as I jerked the strap tight. Sweating with fear and not able to look at her, I felt the leather thong bite in.

My body shuddered, appalled. There was no way I could find some similar device for Ellen. Composure shot to pieces, I staggered across to my horse and leaned on its warm breathing flank, the smell of it being indescribably wholesome.

The truth hit me, as I fitted the strap round her neck, that Norah never loved me in any way except with the maternal love of a sister for a younger brother. Really, I'd known since the previous day when I caught sight of them emerging from that ravine as a couple. Just the way they turned together, as one, and raised their arms to shade their eyes against the lowering light, I knew, and possibly Ellen in my arms for protection against spears knew also, that they were not trying to pick us out for our sake. They were simply and completely doing something together. They were celebrating their escape, not just from whatever sinister event we had interrupted where puddles of blood still lay wet on the stone, not just from the rule of law at home, Pa's violence and Mum's resentment, but from us . . . from, when you come down to it, me.

To a Murphy, you see, no matter how sordid our lives may appear on the outside, Paradise contained the full variety of human richness. Not its fullest possible extent, of course, no single life can offer that; but whatever one may conceive as valuable and contributing to the majesty of mankind's unique opportunity in the world had its expression in some or other particular within our family. However small, the glints of enlightenment seemed precious to us. Kindness which could defy Pa's wrath had a heroic cast difficult to match in any situation since the days of convict labour. Virtues and sins were known to us, often in intensified form, as that surrender of personal expression so close to the heart of the monastic ages when dedicated martyrs achieved an ecstasy envied by laxer eras.

The brutalities of our life at Paradise, the blind rules and desperate suppression were all in their own way moral. Yes, and most moral where most wrong. You will think me perverse for saying so, but the grimmest peaks of suffering, those feelings of being most hopelessly trapped, are the times I hold precious as I look back on them. Whatever else, they were not tainted with the contemptible blandness, the utterly grey indifference and suffocating comfort now fallen like a blanket on the whole country. I accept what this, ultimately, means. I have no wish to throw it in anyone's face, but my view of life has been cast on a huge scale by the sin I committed against my own blood. If hell exists and I am damned for what I did, I accept the price.

I wonder, did it occur to you, too, that I might have smashed Michael's skull partly from anger? You see, Norah may, just may, have shot him for what *I* had done to her, shot him because this would not simply be justice (as shooting *me* would be) but an act glorifying her revenge with outrage adequate to the crime already com-

mitted against her body. If so, it might account for the
look in Ellen's eyes: Ellen, who had at last and only then
come face to face with a recognition of evil.

I rode the lame horse for some of the way to confirm
this God-given lameness. Also to get clear as quickly as
I was able, because someone must have heard the screams.
I could not risk any further time checking details. As
events transpired, I made only one mistake. I lost a small,
an unimportant object: a Saint Christopher medal Father
Gwilym had once given me in a moment of enthusiasm
for my progress at managing to recite the *Dies Irae*
complete and without pause. As this was the first gift I
had ever received from any person outside Paradise, I
treasured the medal far beyond its actual worth as an
object, or apparently its symbolic worth as a protection
against accidents! By habit I kept it in my pocket.

Late that night when I undressed in my room, in the
respectable captivity I had thought to escape, with Willie
—having arrived well before me to face the hostilities of
a turbulent household—snoring against the wall, docile
as ever, I did not think to put it under my pillow. I was
too agitated to pick up the threads of normality. I did not
miss it. Not even next morning. Not even by the time
Arthur Earnshaw galloped in at our gate, flinging himself off his big gelding and rushing headlong, deferen-
tial but unstoppable, into the main room to confront
Pa the giant and his giant consort with news that their
offspring had been murdered in his dad's bottom paddock, and stood there confounded by their lack of any-

thing to respond with, outraged by their failure to be moved, nor knowing (as how could he know?) that life had not taught them anything with which they might make sense either of such an intrusion or of such loss.

They were homespun giants, my mother and father. There was a time when I thought them filled with a wisdom they had no ability to pass on. There was also a time when I thought them completely successful in imposing their own laws, however these might contravene the laws outside our boundary fence. But now I see them as people so reclusive as to have been almost in hiding.

Maisie O'Donovan (one of the violin girls through all the years from church to the hall dances) told me much later that the photographer Charles Bailey of Bunda had proposed to her parents, who were shorter people than average, that for a consideration of ten shillings, which he would pay them, he would be pleased to have them agree to a joint portrait with Mr and Mrs Daniel Murphy at Paradise. Just a photograph of good neighbours, Bailey said. So his coming and using our twenty for that first try at *Caught Unawares* might not have been as innocent as it seemed. Did he hope by this contact and by making one corner of our property famous enough to sell in public, he could smooth his way to propose the real treasure of his imagination, a further essay into the bizarre life of the district entitled *Ogres and Gnomes*, perhaps? Was my mother's time at church, at the rare fête or race meeting, wholly taken up in an agony of self-consciousness about her colossal size? Every pleasure poisoned by needing to assess how freakish the most ordinary behaviour must appear on such a scale? Not until she had been dead some years did it occur to me that the answer to Mum's riddle might be shyness—shy about her six feet eight inches, for all its grace, shy about her lack of education, about our family reputation, also wishing to keep private from the world for fear of Pa breaking out into violence? Perhaps she was, in this way at least, a benefactor to the community.

Sheer bulk could hardly have been such an embarrassment for a man. Had Pa, then, surrendered his liberty to be with her? Did he prove she was normal by not seeming any more eager than herself to mix with other parishioners? Now I think back, I remember, behind the refreshment tent at the Yandilli racetrack, children's peeping heads spying on the monsters at their picnic; I see their gasping faces, their pink excitement, the star of an open hand being clapped across its owner's face as a gesture beyond words. In much the same spirit, Mum had prevented Willie going out, after his brains had been rattled loose. If she let him be seen, even on the road, folk might treat him as an idiot or investigate how he came to change. So, though he grew to be almost unknown among our neighbours for most of his adult life, she may not have asked any more of him than of herself.

The judgments we make depend largely on the way we view things in the first place. I used to think Mum's choice of a bead curtain, as expressing her ideal for our home, was some kind of lapse from native austerity. I now

see it as an image of the essential woman: light-catching
and frail.

Another fact which must be told in this history concerns
Pa. After his name was cleared by the magisterial enquiry,
and when scores of other suspects had all disproved al-
legations of guilt against them, an ugly determination
arose in Cuttajo to find a scapegoat. I have already spoken
of the Aboriginal tribe still haunting the hills hereabouts.
Well, the rumour went that they had been interrupted in
the middle of a heathen ceremony the previous day and
had taken revenge. It was said that these people still ini-
tiated their young into savage practices they ought to
have outgrown long years before, that they speared the
occasional (always valuable) sheep for feasts culminat-
ing in weird cries and chants which they sent winding
down the ravine toward civilization such as we knew it,
unsettling our dogs to a frenzy of barking.

One autumn morning, mist stirring around the horse's
hocks, Pa rode out on hearing that justice would at last
be seen to be done. I followed him, as ever. He—whom
these blacks had watched year after year setting up the
Kilkenny frame for crucifying a Christmas pig—might
now (had the news arrived in time for them to come
down and stand invisible among the trees as only they
know how) see him ride out on his kingly black stallion,
towering above that rabble and their heat of justice—he
who never spoke of the tribe his own father dispossessed
unless to dismiss them as shiftless, made a speech fine

enough to have belonged in *Lives of the Saints.* He (whom this journal might release from his vigil, while also granting his wife's shade the peace she vainly seeks behind cupboards, under tables, even on the far side of people's faces) floated on cloud through our gate, where PARADISE had been burnt in wood by young Daniel before joining the constabulary. His coat winged out on either side, the fortress of his great sadness thrown open to marauders, and the way to his soul stood for once unguarded.

"I am the one who bears the wound," he asserted as he rode up out of the mist to block their furtherance with his determination. "The wound is not yours but mine to bear. Though not an easy man to know, there is strength in my heart and my blood. My heart is strong. Harsh I have been, but never false. I can face the fact that you are doing this for me. I can face the insult of it and the kindness. We are not a thinking breed. But when we have nothing more than habit to support us, then the habit of peace is a treasure. I do not say we are bound to put some curb on ourselves when we feel we are doing what is right, I only say that a curb is something we understand, but knowing what is right is better left to God."

His horse sidled a few steps and presented the other flank. His hand lay huge and reassuring on its neck as he faced them again, offering the left cheek.

"Are we to climb into hills," he continued, "where we have never set foot? Hasn't one Mystery been enough?"

He took off his tall hat and set it on the pommel between his thighs. The horse felt then, as animals will, what the moment of grace required, and stood steady as the dead, sensing the humiliator humiliated.

On that autumn morning, when Pa spoke of the wounds as his and claimed strength for his heart at the very moment of exposing its weakness; when he, our absolute dictator of what was right, surrendered this privilege to God, I knew how we had come to the pass we had. My throat betrayal-clogged, fury welled painfully through me.

I looked from one face to another, all complacent in stupidity, some from the stupidity of kindliness and some callous. How had they gathered, these fourteen riders riding here to assemble fourteen incompatible pasts, bringing fourteen lost boys scolded by fatuous wheedling forthright mothers, fourteen memories of fathers whom they might once have supposed rivalled mine in his special standing with the universe, two of whom I knew as active Federalists, six as Christians of our own ilk, the rest as Protestants, except one Jew who had no religion the way we understood religion, which is to say something separate from the rest of his humdrum life. I put the age of the youngest at nineteen and the oldest at sixty, so it was neither headstrong ambition nor world-bitterness that lured them. Their horses shuffled in a shifting clump, some passing behind others, some tugging at reins to investigate the road for fodder, some whisking flies or opening their lids to show each other dangerous sickles of their intentions, stamping, anxious to be off; the milder

beasts meanwhile—hoping this inaction might promise
a companionable walk back home to the fixed social
priorities of a paddock properly fenced, and time for
philosophy beyond the taint of usefulness—sagged on
their fetlocks. What had brought such riders out in
their horrifying ignorance? To look into their eyes was
to see only contemptibly domestic issues, small worries,
and capability cramped by lack of challenge. The men
did not move, drifting among one another, their concentration never deflected from Pa. Only the horses moved,
muffled drums trembling through haunches, manes
shaking and the sky gauzed across their glossy vision.

Pa, with his iron grief, held the party of their retribu-
tion magnetized. Wrong as they were, they should have
gone on; their self-esteem demanded that at least, none
being man enough to actually think a matter through. I
could not have conceived such timidity: this one a hoary
freckled lad and famous still for pranks; this one, who
became adult at twelve to fend for a family, and lost his
high heart in the thicket of habitual bullying; this one,
keeping to the rear, blank yet watchful under a broad-
brimmed hat; this one smirking, already on his treadmill
of excuses; the fellow with a pottery nose and cured
leather cheeks, wire beard, sleeves pushed up from thick
ropey forearms and from the curse of hands, thighs hardening and outsized genitals bagged in loose trousers, who
must have felt all pleasure drain from expectation while
his neighbours' resolve began to fail; this other, who
went to Athens competing as a jumper in the first Olym-

pic games for sixteen centuries, now facing a future of
local adulation he need never do another thing to earn;
this one charmed with lack of bloodlust, despair of his
generations; this fat whiskered elder extracting pipe and
tobacco pouch which, in itself, signalled that the business
of arms had become a business of the intellect; this
tough and handsome timber cutter scratching at his skull
as if he might dig out an idea of his own; this clan of
worriers, escapees from the routines they'd chained themselves to. Their lives hung round them, sloppy as old
garments worn soft by work and threadbare, faded, and
clotted with the muddy enterprise. Their little eyes shrank
in caves, sly night creatures when it came to talk or thinking what was said; even their shuffling being done for
them by horses knocking nerveless hooves together on the
desolate ground. They had brought along the odours of
shoddy shelters where they'd left anxious wives, the
thinkers of the household, in doubt, and fiercely partisan
youngsters; where the baby, silent at last after a night of
squalling, sat agog at the event, storing impressions that
would later fruit for harvesting in childhood as a crisis
from which its sire might emerge heroic, and an ancient
dusty waistcoat famous. Were these the very men who
volunteered to hunt down the outlawed Ned Kelly,
poachers on the estate of an indulgent judiciary,
sniggering oafs who'd turn and fire the other way out
of anarchist abandon for any whim, but never for an
arguable reason well thought through? With their mix-
ture of self-importance and cruelty, their lust for the

hunt and the illegality of it, their salacious indulgence of collective irresponsibility, they watched Pa. Despite those tireless bodies you could see exhausted souls laid open—finning, suckling, soft mouthparts groping for some comfort to fasten on to, souls as fleshy nodules, primordial organisms in damp places. The parliament of horses nodded and took a step forward, sidled, or exchanged position, rumps brushing, warm nostrils scenting loss of action.

The men had eyes for no one but Pa. They did not understand a word he said. He might as well have addressed them in Arabic. Their fine-tuned measure of power and its fluctuations buzzing alive as an electric charge, they waited only long enough to gauge which way the intuitions of chance would lead them, whether this meant more or less fun or none at all, and already casting in empty hollows of mind for the best tone—how far to contract the eyebrows for indicating decisiveness, an appropriate seat in the saddle for presenting themselves to their wives though unscathed and still untried—plus acknowledging that the future would in all probability grant few such chances. The fellow with the pottery nose, having watched Pa's mouth give out words, was first to look away, contemplating his own grainy forearms hard as logs, even the huge but sinking genitals: he saw only disappointment and thwarted plans, admitting there was nobody he could rely on. Thanks to their holier consciences, their scruples, their spouses, their respectability, their gutlessness (all these being obstacles won over in the festival of setting out from Cuttajo), they would turn back. He signalled his mount to move. And when he moved, so did they, their collective bullish bellicose intention fated to trot home to its stud paddock, too thickly encased in compact flesh to recognize such a backdown as craven.

Pa reviewed his victory. But I flamed at the disgrace, at his furling our standard and bundling away the pennants and favours of so many campaigns in order to plead with that rabble. How could he renounce the pride of our elite by showing his heart to cattle, offering them words he never offered us in all our faithful years—these locals whose tame superstitions had baffled even Father Gwilym's efforts to civilize them? Pa jammed his crown back on his head and faced me, perhaps for confirmation that he was in the right. I might have wept. This was worse than the rest. My disenchantment beyond concealing, he saw what he saw.

We rode home side by side, together and apart in our isolation.

Being drawn towards the shore by a force as invisible as willpower, Artie Earnshaw and I stood on deck among other diggers returning home via Sydney on the coastal steamer. We watched well-known headlands loom in their nether aspect of a seaman's view, those shaggy topknots of scrub grown dense on rock so disused it had rotted. Engines beneath us thumping and pulsing, twin funnels spouted plumes to hang in the air above our laboured progress. A mat of soot sank, from time to time, to choke us, and then lifted its frayed feathers, hovering, a giant bird slightly beyond the steamer but always in reach. We watched Cuttajo wharf appear as a finger of civilization pointing out into Cuttajo Bay, and the closer we drew, the more inevitable the crowd of miniature colours clustered on its top and bottom tiers, sunlight streaming down to break as a surf of tiny white handkerchiefs waving. Beyond our powers of resistance, like some appallingly logical conclusion to the wildernesses of nightmare called France and Flanders, we had earned our homecoming—a lesson in the truth that one cannot escape one's origins, or even outgrow them. I nearly spoke of this to Artie, but caught his shining expression of a true victor in reach of laurels.

"Home, eh?" I said.

He included me in the loving breadth of his smile, but could not find the voice to speak.

I hung over the side and watched the last fatal chasm of deep water slip harmlessly beneath us, our shadow forcing its cold blunt passage across submerged rocks, driving schools of fish before it, arriving like the carcase of some blind force washed in towards marvelling watchers, as incapable of not arriving as they were of fending it off, gliding, bumping, and swinging broadside to the wharf. Timbers yelped and groaned too late and a chuckle of water escaped among the pylons, wagging beards of weed. Only then did I look up, because I supposed I had to face my welcome.

On the top tier, just above head level, my reception party hovered over me in the full blaze of afternoon, all but Jeremiah leaning out from the rail, orifices gaping, dentures gnashing to chop the separate words of greeting into bleeding parts, hands open eager to acquire my head, to grasp the hair and drag me up among them or push me under. Voices tempting me in the laconic vernacular of Paradise, celebrating my survival even while I shrank from contact.

Then Artie slapped me on the shoulder and my vision jumped to the shaded lower tier, where his five youngsters (the eldest boy, who went to Melbourne to enlist, just as the war ended, had stayed there) and that nice placid wife watched him with adoring eyes already clouded by concern at what the closer focus showed them of the world he brought from places where they had been told our history was made. They were the ones I called hullo to. And, briefly, they were distracted from the shock of knowledge to wonder who I was.

The blind beast, lashed firmly fore and aft, strained against its bonds. That was the moment when, still gazing into dim recesses of the lower tier, with its slashes of brilliance slicing from between the decking above, I thought of Danny—Daniel junior, still back there, festering in a mass grave called duty, buried in trench-mud, mute and inglorious indeed, and I knew his death was meaningless. He had died so that the whole carnage itself might *remain* meaningless, he died to oblige the rich, to persuade all who knew him that the war had been personal. In this conspiracy, the gamblers did careful sums, no question about that, they multiplied our Danny by eight million dead and multiplied that by at least five relatives close enough to be persuaded. Forty million acceptances, they reckoned, ought to buffer them sufficiently from any irresponsible backlash, at least till next time. You could not argue with it. My brother's death alone made argument obscene. Only at that moment, already too late, I glanced up again towards the welcomers who had come to fetch me, finding myself channelled ashore by comrades and pushed straight into the clutches of Katie, who repelled me with kisses as if nothing had happened in my world which had not also happened in hers, and to Johnnie, clowning to hide his chagrin at not having had the guts to make it to the front before the whole adventure squealed to a halt. Unable to account for why I had returned at all, I took refuge in shaking hands with Jeremiah, already in his wheelchair and grown smaller, lighter—even his bones wasting away and soon to be not much thicker than my own.

"How are you, old son?" I said, and these were my first words to the family. The stroke, I saw immediately, had taught Jerry not to presume anything. Now we had at least this much understanding in common.

Polly was too busy with her Mack, also returning on that steamer, to spare me more than a passing fragment of her world as it flew apart:

"And what's more, I said to Mrs Halligan—you wouldn't know her, Patrick, she's new to the district, I hope your wounds are healed Pat, that's the spirit—the whole point is a question of the jam judge, I said, the jam has to be judged above suspicion, our good name depends upon it, but Mack it does, or we shall see the annual show go down the drain with so many others and this we must never . . ."

The blind beast had been unbound to sigh and sag away from the firm structure of our arrival, to drift bereft and used; so soon after rocking us in its care, so soon after

being the extent and confinement of this life, so soon after
delivering us to fate, it was seen to dwindle, to sail
beyond reach, repelled with disturbing swiftness, reduced
and vulnerable, an ugly little craft, unsafe, an impertinent
object, an intruder on that glittering expanse—even its
smoke smudge cleared away quickly and was lost. We
were left with a blank of missing years. We would never
retrieve what we had missed, or shed the burden of what
we had done. Between us and our youth yawned a ravine.
(When I look again at the view from the high tip of that
other ravine, far away beyond Michael and Norah's doll-
like figures, hadn't there been another person also shading
his eyes against the sun to watch me embrace Ellen, a
dour witness scuffing among broken reeds lower down the
creek, leaving unmistakable footprints? And yet, on second thought, mightn't the dourness itself be my habitual
error in seeing only what I accepted as explicable?
Mightn't he have turned to climb back through the fence,
heavy with power, exultant that his plot worked so perfectly with only the slightest prod from himself in the
timely refusal to accompany us? Even as he had leaned
on the verandah rail, wearing an expression of hostile
suspicion, making certain we saw him, had he been busy
behind the mask, suppressing anxieties that we might
prove fallible as usual and break, scattering like idiotic
sheep to frustrate even the cleverest and most patient of
shepherds?) I did, at length, face William.

To my surprise I knew, in that instant of acknowledging my eldest brother, what it felt like to confront the

faceless men. All through the Great War we had sworn
vengeance against them. Once we hid before the artillery
onslaught and knew the enemy hid before ours in a stale-
mate none but a hero could fight free of, and then only
in flashes of suicidal abandon, the whole conspiracy
slotted into place. While German soldiers and Allied soldiers remained locked in helpless combat, brokers on both
sides were free to go about their importances of angling,
slipping into evening suits and complaining that the oy-
sters tasted two days old, minds clear of distractions and
exultant in this clarity, composing symphonies of pure
mathematics.

Poor pathetic Willie did not appear to recognize me
with any certainty, yet his eyes were surprised to a silver
ripple of closing steel and glass.

How had I never recognized him as the new man, in
tranquil offices, signing yet another promise with his
executive pen, speaking by telephone or buzzing secre-
taries? I had been too much a creature of last century to
guess that dominion was gone from such simplicities as
clearing scrub and planting potatoes, from an empire of
defeating sons, or even chaining them to the bed. Our
worn-out heraldries had mouldered to a dumbshow of
tatters; even the sewers of the defeated civilization were
walled up—and price-tags dangled from sacred images.
The new man did not go underground with silly Corporal
Daniel Murphy, who would never be promoted and was
lost as soon as mud clutched his knees and refused to let
him stagger out lest whole communities might get the

idea they could question why so many lives needed to be put to the bullet. The new man created a modern order out of nothing more than his lameness.

As for us, we never ceased to recall the recent past of slugging away with our rifles. Our ears were still clubbed numb, and our shoulders jolted. We never ceased to recall our jubilation when scoring a bull's-eye and watching a man fall, to know ours was the bullet that brought him down—do you think there was any difference between this jubilation and nausea?

Now the steamer had vanished, dragging its hot oil smell and the lingering throb of its heart. For a brief spell the shore-bound boots' surprised clatter also stilled. In this clearing air, a violin band could at last be heard on the fourth repeat of "Land of Hope and Glory," while surviving heroes clasped lovers and children in their arms. Yes, now and for a whole month, we could expect to be treated as heroes, till people lost the energy to pretend they knew what we had done.

Willie was the one who mattered. He took that terrible blow from Pa, which I saw as my oil-lamp flared in the wind of their passage, to teach the old man he should never completely lose himself in violence again. Without Willie, the rest of us may not have walked straight either. I accepted his hand and understood that this was why I chose to stay. This was the Ireland of my youthful captivity, which I, like Saint Patrick, must embrace again with the faith I had learned in France. I must at the same time love and defeat him. Pride gave me no choice.

Historical Note

ⱴ ⱴ ⱴ

In the cemetery at Gatton, in southern Queensland, stands a monument:

IN MEMORY

OF

MICHAEL, Aged 29 Years.

NORAH, Aged 27 Years.

ELLEN, Aged 18 Years.

The dearly beloved children of

DANIEL and MARY MURPHY,

of Tenthill,

who were the victims of a horrible

tragedy perpetrated near Gatton

on December 26th, 1898.

REQUIESCANT IN PACE.

This Monument has been erected by public

subscription to the memory of the

above innocent victims.

The unsolved mystery of the Gatton murders has been carefully researched and written about in a book by James and
Desmond Gibney, *The Gatton Mystery* (Angus & Robertson,
1977). For the purposes of my novel, I have used the actual
names of the victims and their family; William McNeil, the
butcher and husband of Polly Murphy; Sergeant Arrell; the
government medical officer Dr von Lossberg; and the Brian
Boru Hotel. The distances from the farm to the race meeting in
one direction, and to the township in the other, are the same,
as are the times involved in the crime, plus the testimony of
witnesses who passed the victims' sulky on the road and heard
screams in the night.

Details of the condition of the murdered bodies, where and
how they were found, with feet pointing west, is as described
on pages 3 and 5 of *The Gatton Mystery*; the account of the
stranger at the sliprail is on page 70; the screams heard by
Louisa Theuerkauf and Catherine Byrne on pages 77 and 78;
and the newspaper headlines from the *Toowoomba Chronicle*
of 29th December 1898 on page 2.

All else is my invention. The action has been transferred to
a hypothetical farming district in New South Wales. The character of the persons involved, their physical appearance, the
settings, conversations, motives, and confessions are fictitious.

R. H.
Barragga Bay, August 1986